FROST GIANT LOKI

LIZA PENN

NATASHA LUXE

FROST GIANT LOKI

BESTSELLING AUTHORS

Liza Penn and Natasha Luxe

PROLOGUE: FAITH

stretch languidly on the bed. "It's hard to think that this is the end."

Daniel slides out from the sheets, heading to the shower. He barely grunts in agreement with me, but I'm used to the way it takes a steaming hot shower and a big cup of coffee to actually wake him up.

As steam billows out of the open bathroom door, I sit up, adjusting myself to the weird view of the mostly barren room. I moved in with Daniel for the last year of grad school, and although it had seemed a little risky to share an apartment with my boyfriend without a back-up plan, it had worked wonderfully. We shared our bed and our research, and now we are going to walk across the stage today, accept our doctorates, and — hopefully — also accept the grant that will fund our proposal.

I allow myself one moment to dream of what will come. The Loki Project has been my goal since I was in high school. What started out as a fan girl crush on various iterations of Loki in the media turned into a full-blown academic interest in the *real* Loki of history. I was surprised to learn how little archaeological evidence of Loki exists. He's the original man of legend, and I'm going to find him. Or at least as many artifacts as I can dig up in Scandinavia.

I flop back on the pillows, wishing I could luxuriate in bed before the graduation ceremony. A loophole in the lease means we have to move out early. As in, *today* early. My car is already loaded with my clothes and stuff, with nothing more than a dress for today and my graduation gown hanging in the closet. Daniel's buddies are coming over later to help move out the bed and the couch and the other things that required a pick-up to move. The plan is for me to couch surf with my friends and him to stay at his parents' house upstate until we make arrangements for our very own Viking quest. It's not ideal, but it's a hassle that will be more than worth the while when we board the plane together in a few weeks.

Daniel's shower is taking forever, so I get up and slip my dress over my head. Lingering at the closet, I run my hand over the black graduation gown, the little lines of false fur indicating my doctoral status. "Dr. Faith Beck," I whisper, relishing the sound of it. "Lead Historian on the Loki Project."

The grant isn't going to be awarded until graduation, but Dr. Phillips told me privately that it was going to win. She wasn't on the board for it — she had to recuse herself when I told her I was applying, so she wouldn't be biased in my favor — but she'd overheard the board talking about it.

The folio with our application is on the shelf in the closet above Daniel's graduation robe. With the apartment emptied, there's nothing to do until Daniel's out of the shower. I grab the folio, flipping it open, not bothering to read the words I've labored over for more than a year.

I could join him in the shower . . . The thought has me pausing. It's been a hot second since we had a good time in bed together. I mean . . . the ten minutes last night was okay, but not exactly the monumental send-off for the evening before graduation I'd been expecting. Daniel's been weird for the past few weeks — nerves from the move, worries about prepping for the next move to Norway for our project. Maybe we both need to really focus on some physical relief.

I start to put the folio back on the shelf, already

half-turning to head into the shower with him, when I see Daniel standing in the doorway. I hadn't heard the water cut off.

He has a towel around his waist, his hair wet, and seeing his chest like that, muscles hard from research digging in the field, his towel slipping off his narrow hips . . . all that is usually enough for me to throw myself at him, but his expression now is filled with an unreadable dark look. "What are you doing?" he asks too harshly.

"Nothing?" Something about his tone puts me on edge.

I look down at the folio in my hand, the copy of the papers we submitted to the board. There's nothing inside that should rankle him.

"Faith, I — " he starts, but I'm already flipping the papers open, reading the words on the page.

The cover page has our signatures. There's his name scrawled over the title 'Lead Archeologist.' My name beside his, 'Lead Historian.' Daniel had accidentally spilled coffee over the grant allocation page, and we'd had to rush to reprint it and get it submitted on time. I remember the way the paper had still been warm from the printer when I signed it.

I remember not re-reading the paper before I added my signature.

I read it now, as Daniel stands in the bathroom door, dripping wet and a look of horror filling his face.

I read how the funds are to be divided.

The majority of the grant money — two-hundred and fifty thousand dollars — is to go to Daniel.

One thousand dollars is to go to me.

That won't even buy a plane ticket to Norway.

"What the fuck," I mutter. I grip the papers as I meet Daniel's shame-filled eyes. "What the *fuck?*" I shout.

"I didn't cut you out entirely," Daniel says, as if that makes it better.

"A *thousand?*" I shake my head, realization washing over me. "You threw me the bare minimum because of the paper trail," I say. "If you'd cut me out entirely, everyone would have known you scrubbed me from the grant, and it wasn't fair. But you gave me a handout so it looked legit. Everyone in the department knows I worked on this grant."

"You don't have to be mad," he says. "This is going to be great. Getting this grant will mean the Gloucester Group will hire me. That's the job of a lifetime. You can still come. Be my researcher . . ."

"Books." I shake my head. I love books, I love research, but I don't want to *only* lock myself into a library while Daniel does the field research. "You don't want a girlfriend or a partner," I spit back at him. "You want a secretary."

I toss the papers at his feet, watching as water from his shower drips on them. It doesn't matter. That folio contained a Xeroxed copy of the papers already submitted — and approved — by the grant board. In a few hours, Daniel will walk across the stage and accept both his doctorate and the grant. A quarter of a million dollars. With a funnel into a job at one of the biggest archeology firms in the world.

And me?

He really thought he could string me along with nothing more than a thousand dollars and the promise of books.

"You don't need the field work like I do," Daniel said, his tone pleading. "All you cared about was the mythology and legends. But I need to dig. I need to uncover the artifacts."

I stare at him. Of course, I love the legends. I know them all by heart. The stories about the Norse gods — the legendary heroes, the untouchable gods. Everyone knows Thor and Odin, but the pantheon is broken into tribes, with epic mythology spinning and twisting for centuries like the gnarled roots of Yggdrasil, the sacred tree.

"You only care about Loki, like some fangirl,"

Daniel continued. "I need to find *real* artifacts to be considered for the Gloucester Group."

"Our grant is for the *Loki Project*, you fucking tool!" I scream at him, throwing my arm toward the drenched papers. "Of course I was focused on Loki!"

"Still, Faith, you have to admit — "

"I don't have to fucking do anything," I snarl. "Except leave."

Daniel reaches for me, his towel dropping. Naked, wet, hurt, but still, somehow, wanting to gaslight me into being his library intern. I let my eyes rake over his body — a body I had fucked just the night before, the lying traitor — and I let my full disgust at everything he is show. "Níðingr," I hiss at him, knowing full well that while most people at our university wouldn't comprehend the curse, he understands I'm calling him the most vile slur I can think of in Viking lore, a nothing-man who contributes no good to the universe, only evil.

I spin around, grabbing the only thing in the room worth anything to me — my graduation robe, hanging in the closet. I yank it so hard, though, that it rips, one full sleeve dangling by nothing but threads.

Screaming in rage, I throw it on the floor at his feet and storm out of the apartment.

CHAPTER 1
FAITH

Maya places a mug down in front of me, sliding over a hefty slice of death-by-chocolate cake. Before I can say anything, she piles on a load of fresh, handmade whipped cream and starts shaving a dark chocolate bar on top of the mound.

"This much sugar is going to make me sick," I tell her, but I still pick up a fork, ready to dive in.

"That's why I put rum in the coffee," she says. "Balances the sweet."

That math doesn't quite check out, but I don't care. I dive in, not even pretending to protest when she tops my mug off with more rum, sans the pretense of coffee.

Maya is far too good to me — to all my friends. She's like a school mom to us all, students and professors alike. Her old, gated Victorian home had once been a boarding house, and she talks all the time about turning it into a bed and breakfast. The ground floor has been renovated into a café, and the back room, an ancient library that spills into a formal study and a screened-in back porch, is permanently reserved for the Study Group.

It doesn't matter what major you're in. The Study Group is a safe place to focus on the things we love, from history to science. While it may have started strictly academic, it's shifted into a social group that's laid the foundation for lifelong friendships.

I have no idea who the first members of the Study Group were. Perhaps Dr. Phillips, when she was an undergrad? Going to one of the most elite, competitive universities in the nation meant an uphill battle as it was, but add to that the male-dominated fields the school specializes in, and it's little wonder that the women started to band together.

The boys have their frats and their secret societies and their exclusive little clubs. They have legacies and alumni support and sports funding.

We have the Study Group.

And we have Maya. "Bless you," I say as she takes away my empty plate.

"Figured you deserved a little extra," she says. "Amie told me what happened."

Amie — Dr. Phillips — has been more than just a mentor to me during my grad studies. She was the one who ensured I knew about the Study Group; she told me about the grant program. And she was the first person I called, crying in my car in a McDonald's parking lot, after my dramatic exit from Daniel's apartment.

I push the thought from my mind. I have to find a way to do the Loki Project on my own, without Daniel or the grant. The without Daniel part I can handle, but the lack of funds is a serious problem. I need to actually go to Scandinavia. My theories all revolve around finding the mythological location of Jotunheim.

To the Greeks, the gods lived on Mount Olympus. And that mountain wasn't some made-up place in the sky — there is a literal mountain in Greece called Mount Olympus, and linking the mythology to the location was key for archeological discoveries. My theory — which Daniel always thought was idealistically dumb — is that Jotunheim is a real physical place the ancient Vikings had ascribed to Loki. It was the land of the giants, and who is more giant than a god? There was just enough evidence in the poetry and the legends for me to link Loki and Jotunheim; and I was hoping to find the evidence in archeology to link them both to a specific island in the Arctic Ocean.

The bell on the front door of the cafe tinkles. "Ah, there they are," Maya says.

"Who?" I turn in my seat. With no apartment to go back to, I hadn't had the courage to face my friends and tell them how royally fucked I am. I don't want to ruin their graduation, too. I had planned to drown my sorrows in cake and rum until tomorrow, after the celebrations and parties were done.

Instead, I see more than half of the Study Group arriving. "What are you guys doing here?" I ask as a dozen girls pour into the room.

"Eh, it's just a boring ceremony," Ellie said.

Cate gives me a hug. "Dr. P told me to tell you that she's starting an inquiry."

I nod, choked up. I know Dr. Phillips is going to look into the grant, but at the end of the day, I signed the wrong paper. I can't deny that I signed it. And if I push too hard . . . well, I know how it'll look to the prestigious archeological firms. There is a solid chance I can get justice on this, but it would come at the expense of my future career.

I look around at them all. The Study Group is more of a family than I've known for years. Collected in this room are the best and brightest women in archeology, classical studies, architecture, and more.

Some are graduating today, like me; some have their doctorates already and work at the university or in the city; some are still undergrads.

All are friends. And they all came to me when I needed friends the most.

"Don't cry!" Josie says, rushing over. "Would it help if we kicked his ass? I would happily kick his ass."

"It might," I say.

Josie grins in a feral way.

"I mean, not murder," I add quickly.

"How much not murder?"

"Not murder at all!" I say. "Daniel's not worth a felony."

"It's only a felony if you get caught." Josie turns on her heel, heading to the table with cake and booze Maya is quickly setting up.

"Don't!" I call after her.

She raises a hand without pausing. "Don't get caught, got it."

Marie sidles up to me. "I'll keep an eye on her."

"Thanks."

Cate and Renee exchange a glance at my tone. "So, Daniel is a total dick," Cate says.

"Obviously." Josie passes out mugs of rum.

"But he only has the money," Cate continues. "You have the brains. You'll be able to do far more."

"I can't even get to Norway," I say. "Maybe, if he'd at least brought me along, we could have gone our separate ways, and I could have made a name for myself. We did clash on some of our theories." For one, Daniel never believed I could find Jotunheim. Or that it would lead me to real Loki artifacts. He wanted to focus on a dig that was already established, not find a new one.

Music starts up. Maya has closed the cafe to everyone but us, and it's turning into a regular party. I have to admit, it's far better now than the solitary pity party I had been throwing myself. And even though guilt nags at me that my friends are missing the graduation ceremony, I'm so grateful that they chose me instead.

"You clashed on your theories because he has no vision," Renee says. "Honestly, I'm surprised he had enough brains to trick you."

"Well, he did." I was wrong. I want to wallow alone.

"Go anyway." Dr. Phillips's voice cuts across the music. She's in her full regalia, from the tip of her hat to her black robe lined in fur.

"Aren't you supposed to be conducting the graduation ceremony?" I ask, gaping at her.

Dr. Phillips shrugs. "What are they going to do, fire me?" She strides across the room, and the other girls part in her wake. Even the ones who don't have her as their advisor know and respect Dr. Phillips. And maybe Dr. Phillips is going to piss off the dean by skipping the graduation ceremony, but she's the most beloved professor on the campus who brings in more connections than anyone. No one has as much power as she does, even the men in the higher paid positions above her. She's untouchable.

"It was a shit thing he did," she tells me in a low voice. "But he is nothing."

"Níð," I repeat, using the Old Norse word. She nods, a little smile on her face. She went for the same insult I had thrown at Daniel. She really does understand how deep this cut went.

And she is right. Daniel is nothing. That's what made the curse so powerful. Death, to a Viking, is a pathway to immortality and honor. A hero who died a hero's death is hailed in the halls of Valhalla. But a nothing-man?

It's like he never existed at all.

Dr. Phillips looks down her nose at me, a challenge in her eyes. "So?" she says. Everyone in the room watches us, and I feel all their love and support.

"So, I'm going to Norway anyway," I announce. I'll have to max out every credit card I have, but . . .

I'm going.

CHAPTER 2
LOKI

The hall is in fine form tonight. Dozens of bodies pack the massive room, all of them burly and thick, blue skin glistening in the exertion of drink and the pulse of firelight. Fire for light only; most of the giants before me are barely dressed, wrapping furs and leathers placed strategically, but otherwise they are lost in revelry, as always.

As it should be.

"Drink!" comes the chant, bolstered by voices that echo off the high wooden rafters.

"For peace and pledge!" comes the answer, and dozens of tankards tip back in gulps of golden liquid.

"Drink!" half the voices chant again.

"For ale and eating!" A boisterous *huzzah* always follows that one; more tankards tip.

"Drink!"

"For steel and horn!"

"Drink!" Sigyn elbows me in the side as he joins the final chant, his white eyebrows rising in insistence.

Anyone else would get a death glare; but Sigyn's wizened features leave me rolling my eyes and lifting my tankard.

"For dreams far fleeting!" I call out as the room does. More than a few eyes swivel toward me at the sound of my voice. Cheers and whistles pepper the air. Some applaud and call for more barrels.

Sigyn gives me a satisfied nod. "That will appease them," he murmurs.

Is it really so infrequent that my people see their leader partaking in their revelry?

I swallow a mouthful of the bitter ale and continue my survey of the evening. From the rear table, it isn't hard — a strategic position for the highest lords of Jotunheim positioned above the crowd, but more so to see every entrance and exit.

We kept this set-up from times long past, when we needed to always watch for invading enemies.

Such worries should have long faded. I use the position now to keep track of every jostling body that packs this central hall.

I know all of them. Dozens of my people packed together in our nightly union. Their voices ring high, shouts and an overlapping chaos of songs and instruments; noise, noise, such glorious noise that I spent our first few hundred years simply basking in it.

Never again will my people be forced to stifle this joy.

Never again will they be stuffed into castle cellars, breaths held as the stomping of gods hunts them down.

Never again will we fear, or hide, or cower.

That is the purpose of Jotunheim. Our utopia.

Why, then, can I not get that scratch out of the back of my mind, the itch that plagued me every time I was on Earth?

Something is wrong.

Something is coming.

Nothing can touch us here.

I used to partake in our revelry as passionately as my people. Now, it *is* rare that they see their king as he once was — jovial, carefree, buoyant.

But the fear has been growing worse these past years. Creeping over me like a shadow at dusk.

I shift in my fur-lined chair, rolling out a kink in my shoulders.

"Your Highness has no need for preening," Sigyn whispers into his tankard.

I follow his eyes to a row of women near our table. Their own gazes are fixed on my bare chest, the muscles that stretch and pull as I have my arms raised above my head.

I finish my stretch and the three blazing sets of eyes lift to mine. They are all lovely, bodies voluptuous, faces eager, gold bands and strands of greenery woven around their small horns.

I wait for a pull of desire.

None comes.

Fuck.

"Shall I have one brought to you?" Sigyn asks.

"You pry, Sigyn."

"I would never!" He slaps a beefy blue hand to his chest in mock hurt. After a beat, he shrugs. "It is, quite literally, my job to pry apart your life, my liege. How good of a councilor to you would I be if I did not?"

"How often I fuck is no concern of my council's."

"Ah, there you are wrong!" Sigyn leans closer to me, his eyes on the trio of women. "Your people have noticed your . . . solitude, sire. How long has it been since your eyes roamed? A king has power; a king *and* a queen, though . . ."

I feel a wash of his magic attempt to creep over me, if I would allow it. Most frost giants have rudimentary illusory skills — none stronger than mine — but some have smaller abilities. Sigyn has long been a councilor for his ability to quell or inflate emotions.

His ability was immensely useful during battles, against greater gods.

Now, he is trying to push me into seeing his side, albeit good-naturedly.

"Sigyn." I give him a flat stare.

He drops his magic and leans back in his chair, itching the base of his right horn, where it snapped off in a long ago battle. "Think on it is all. A union would go far towards bolstering our people."

That I leap on as a hunter would prey. "They need bolstering? What do you know? What have you heard?"

I *loathe* this worry, but I am helpless to it.

I used to be the epitome of laughter and fun. What am I now? Driven to panic by *nothing*.

Sigyn laughs and slaps my shoulder. "I merely meant that our people adore a chance to celebrate. And what better celebration than the marriage of our king!"

The itch of discomfort, of *wrongness*, does not alleviate.

I turn back to the women, one of whom has been pulled away, commandeered into the lap of my general, Fenrir. He has his tongue deep in her mouth already, the woman's fingers interlaced on his horns; and that is why I felt no stirring of desire.

I know everyone in this room. As a good king

should. I know everyone in the rest of Jotunheim beyond.

I have known them, and watched them, and guided them, for centuries. We have grown here in this utopia I built, this haven locked away from Earth with its monstrous gods who sought only to hunt and abuse my kind.

But the longer we remained here, the less able I have been to see any of these people as *mine* beyond the need to protect them. I know them too well to truly bring one of them to my side, to find my mate.

I sigh, perhaps too loudly, and kick my chair back as I stand. A brief hush falls over those tables closest to mine, and that I do revel in — I know the cutting figure I still make. Tallest of the frost giants, with massive ivory horns that curl back over my long white hair and vibrant blue skin, my shoulders broad and bare chest taut, I can, in these moments, remind them of who I am: Loki, their king and god; Loki, the one who forged their salvation.

I have carried that weight for too long, I think. When was I last just *Loki*, mischief and lightness?

I look down at Sigyn. "I will be in my chambers." *Alone*, I do not add.

Briefly, I consider having Sigyn arrange for one of the women to come to my room. I could do as I have done many times — use my magic to transform them into someone, anyone, new. Willingly, of course; for most, it is a fun game of pretend. Any company would be better than none, would it not?

But the thought has me recoiling. Even if I were to change them, they would not be . . . *her*. The one I feel absent though I do not know.

I long for someone I have never met. I feel the approach of something I cannot see.

It is rattling me.

As I turn to leave, Fenrir leaps to his feet, unceremoniously dumping the lady off his lap. She falls with a cry and her two friends are quick to gather her up.

My eyes flare at him, disgust and anger. Among our magics, Fenrir has a mild ability to peer into the minds of others — so he is not unaware of the hurt that flashes through the woman. He knows, and does not care.

Such callousness makes him brilliant on the battlefield.

But at peaceful feasts . . .

I glare at him. "You dare treat her as if — "

"Our own king grows bored of these parties!" Fenrir bellows, thrusting a tankard my direction. Ale spills over his hand; he's well past drunk already. "He leaves!"

The lady appears unhurt, and so I frown at Fenrir.

"Bored?" One eyebrow lifts. "What precisely is there to be bored of?" I ask it, intending for his answer to be, *Nothing; we have peace, we have everything we could want.*

But I feel the answer resonate deep in my chest. *More. There should be more.*

"Night after night of drinking and song and women," Fenrir waxes, batting his tankard in the air.

I grin. "You are bored of women, Fenrir? Or is it that they have grown bored of you?"

A roar of laughter floods the air.

Fenrir's nose twitches in a scowl. He never did appreciate my humor like he should.

"We are gone soft!" Fenrir tries again. "*Frost giants*, gone soft! Once feared monsters of the mortal realm, now house cats fat on too much milk."

We have drawn the attention of most on this side of the room; the rest carry on in their fun, songs playing, voices laughing. It only serves to back up his words.

"What are you suggesting, Fenrir?" I keep my voice carefully level.

Sobering, he faces me. "Some *fun*," he says, a flash in his eyes.

"Hunting? There are creatures aplenty in Jotunheim to fight and — "

"Not *creatures*. None of this — this *ease*. We were once gods, Loki!"

I huff a laugh. "You want to be worshipped, Fenrir? Back to Earth? Do you not remember who else was worshipped on Earth, and how they felt about sharing altar space?"

Fenrir's face darkens. He slams his tankard onto not his table, but mine, directly beside my discarded plate and cup. "I don't suggest dealing with Odin and his pain in the ass court again. I mean — I mean bringing some of the fun to us! Where's that portal you sealed off? Crack it open, drag a few humans through, and let's relive those days of old and glory!"

He shouts the final word, and a chorus of voices joins him, *huzzah*-ing as strongly as they did during the drinking chant.

I school my features with ease, though inside, my chest bucks with dread. That one of my people would dream of reopening the portal is bad enough; that so many immediately join his side is a disaster.

We *cannot* open the portal.

To open the portal would mean to reconnect with Earth. To reconnect with Earth would mean tempting the eye of feral gods.

We fought too hard, sacrificed too much, for peace here.

Fenrir forgets that.

I plant my hands on the table and vault over it in one smooth move. When I land beside him, thundering on the stone floor, the whole of the long room goes dead quiet.

Fenrir whirls to face me, his eagerness warring with interest, with knowing he struck a nerve. I played that card, at least; but the rest he will never see.

His eyes thin into lines — he is trying to pry into *my* mind, to read *my* thoughts with his magic. I may not possess that ability, but I have long been able to resist him.

"Fun is it you want, Fenrir?" I start, a devilish smile curling my lips. "Then let us have some fun."

I punch him square in the nose.

Fenrir's head snaps back and blood immediately pours down his face, a striking contrast of dark, deep crimson on his pale blue skin. He staggers, but when he looks up at me, he's grinning like the beast he is, the ferocity that makes him such a brilliant general.

But I have been a fool, because what is a general in times of peace? He is bored and dreaming of opening the portal only because I was too short-sighted not to provide him with something to *do*.

This fight will be brief, but it will satiate him; I can see the bloodlust thrumming in his eyes. The crowd has gone back to ecstatic, only now targeted on this fight. Calls go out, bets are placed.

Fenrir lunges for me, spitting blood. I let him get in a punch to my gut, and I rock forward, feigning pain as he drives his knee up and splits my lip. Blood flows, iron and metallic.

For an instant, his fist pulses a strange light; and then he is holding a wicked hammer that he swings towards me.

I do not duck it. Moments before it strikes, I dispel his minor illusion and bat aside his punch. Most frost giants are capable of such parlor tricks, and lesser men would have cowered at the appearance of such a gruesome weapon.

But I am the king of the frost giants.

I lick away the blood and flare my hands.

Around us in this makeshift fighting ring appear four other Lokis. Their heads all tip simultaneously with my own, blood dripping identically down their lower lips, running in a single bead over their pecks, down their stomachs.

The shadow Lokis and I perform five different attacks — one feigns up, one down, one left, one right. Only I go in for the actual hit, waiting a mere second for Fenrir to go dizzy with disorientation. Then I surge on him and thrust my fist up into his chin, popping his head back and up in a sudden, jarring uppercut.

Fenrir goes down, his massive body plummeting to the stones, and the crowd goes absolutely crazed. Screaming, cheering, some good natured boos.

I ignore the lot of them to bend down to Fenrir, who blinks dazedly up at the rafters, and I grab one of his horns.

"If you speak again about opening the portal," I hiss at him, "I will not hesitate to finish what we started here. We have everything we need in Jotunheim; if you are *bored*, we will devise something else for you to do. But do not *ever* let me hear you speak of opening that portal again. We don't need to fuck around with mortals."

Fenrir manages to fix his spinning gaze on me. I cannot read the expression in him; confusion, maybe?

But I do not give him a chance to respond.

I stand and leave the hall, my knuckles burning, the blood drying on my skin.

CHAPTER 3
FAITH

have never spent more money for a more uncomfortable flight. The first plane ticket I could get to Scandinavia — at least the first one I could afford — has me in the middle seat between two beefy guys who believe every armrest in the plane belongs to them but they'll settle for taking both of mine. The air conditioner and the television screen in the seat in front of me are both broken, so by the time I stagger off the plane, I'm sweaty, stinky, and ready to collapse in a pile of frustrated exhaustion.

But then I suck in the crisp, salty air. Copenhagen is still a long way from my final destination, but I've got a stop to make before I go off in my quest to find Loki.

I heft my backpack on my shoulders. I packed

light on purpose, but even as I board the train from the Copenhagen airport to Aarhus, a city to the east of Denmark, I feel weighed down with exhaustion. Thankfully, I have time to catch a nap while the train cuts across the Danish landscape.

I wad up the coat Dr. Phillips got me. It's arctic-grade and much needed. Neon orange so I'll be easy to spot in the snow, the jacket is downy but also waterproof. The inside lining pocket even has a special pad of waterproof paper and a pencil. It was the perfect graduation gift, both practical and considerate. But more than that, it showed Dr. Phillips's faith in me, and *that* is priceless.

Dr. Phillips pulled a few connections to ensure this trip happened — and sponsored the expedition unofficially by sliding several hundred Euros into my pack when I wasn't looking after she dropped me off at the airport. But her connections were the more valuable asset to me. I'm getting a boat in Aarhus, which is taking me to Norway, and then onward to an island that's technically Norwegian but is basically an icy volcano in the Arctic Sea.

First, though? A stop at a museum.

Daniel would have hated this, and that knowledge makes me all the more happy to step inside the Moesgård Museum. For an archeologist, he didn't care about the artifacts people had already found. He had this Indiana Jones idea of archeology, that he would go on adventures and find things no one else ever had . . . which meant he didn't give a fuck about anything already displayed in the museums.

Daniel only cared about the Loki Project because there are so few Loki artifacts in existence. The Moesgård Museum has one of the only identifiable images of Loki — and even that's up for debate. Loki exists in poetry and myth, but images of him?

He's a ghost.

The museum has the Snaptun Stone on display in a glass case. I'm the only one in the room, and I set my backpack down, eagerly leaning in close. The huge rock is carved with a crude face, a triangular chin so sharp that it almost seems like a child's drawing, not an ancient rendering. The only thing that marks this image as possibly Loki are the lips, sewn together in a way that matches the description of his punishment in one of the legends.

Whether Loki is the Marvel version with a green cloak and golden horns or the ancient Viking god, the one thing everyone can agree on is that he has a smart-ass mouth that people want to sew shut.

Still, I love him.

"You're going to prove me right," I tell the stone softly, glad I'm the only one in the room. Although this rock is on display in Denmark, I traced the geology back to a potential Norwegian origin. I narrowed everything down to one specific place — Jan Mayen Island.

And that is where I'm going to find more relics of Loki.

No one's explored Jan Mayen the way I want to. But it's perfect. According to myth, Loki was a source of earthquakes. Jan Mayen is a volcanic island in the Arctic Sea that is also active and a source of earthquakes. It's remote — *very* remote, with no permanent inhabitants.

I found a faint trace of Loki that links him to that volcanic mountain, beyond just the earthquakes and cold. A scrap of poetry, the only record of it fifthhand and translated roughly. The original source is long gone. But I've made bigger bets before, and the poetry just fit so perfectly with my theory:

> *And there he hid from the angry gods*
> *The king of giants*
> *His voice silenced to this world*
> *Under Ullr's water*

Sure, it doesn't mention Loki specifically, and not every legend even links Loki to the giants. But Marvel got that part of the legend right, too, in my opinion — Tom Hiddleston's Loki was originally from a blue-skinned species that was often at war with Asgard. I'm wagering that the "king of the giants" who often angered the Norse gods and had a well-known voice they wanted silenced is Loki.

It was the "Ullr's water" that tripped me up — Ullr is the Norse god of winter, so every article and book that referenced that poem assumed "under Ullr's water" meant under the snow. And, well, Scandinavia has a lot of snow.

But Jan Mayen Island? It has lakes. One of them is called Ullereng Lagoon. And okay, sure, Daniel thinks the word translates from the Norse term for "wool," but it *could* be a reference to Ullr, and . . .

I check my watch.

Only one way to find out.

Time to go.

———

The boat ride to the tiny, private airport is uneventful and cold, and I'm extra glad to have the arctic-grade coat Dr. Phillips gave me. When I get to the airport, I'm also glad I have no more than my backpack on me, because I don't think the plane could have fit more gear. It's so little that I sit in the co-pilot's seat, and I pass my pilot — a lithe woman who looks more like a model than a fly-girl — her coffee.

Even though my transportation continuously gets both smaller and more rugged, nothing prepares me for the icy stretch of land that serves as Jan Mayen Island's air strip. The little prop plane skids to a halt, and the pilot reaches behind her to hand me my pack.

"You sure you got everything you need out here?" she asks me doubtfully.

No. Not at all.

"Definitely," I say.

She goes over some emergency information for me. Although the island's uninhabited, there is a weather and seismic activity outpost here that I have access to, thanks to Dr. Phillips. Still, I know that if something bad happens out here, I'm basically alone. At best, it would take hours to reach me — and that was *if* I made it to the outpost and got the S.O.S. message out.

I grab my pack and carefully get out of the plane. If I thought Copenhagen was cold, it's *nothing* compared to the biting icy wind here. The pilot waves me on, and I step back to a safe distance and watch as she maneuvers the plane around and takes off.

I'm the only person on this icy rock of an island.

Holy shit.

Terror washes over me. I *trained* for this, I knew what it would take. I'm not some amateur.

But every time I went over my pack list or survival methods, every time I did cold training, every time I made a plan . . .

I wasn't alone.

I spend a few hours acquainting myself with the area, starting with the outpost building. It's used by anyone who comes through — scientists, military, communications specialists. While it's well equipped, it's abandoned now. I locate the emergency radio. I log in a life check and status. I check the maps and the time — it'll be dark soon, but I'm pretty sure I can make it to Ullereng Lagoon before things get close to dangerous.

I step outside. It's still early, but the sky is already darkening. "I just want to see it," I tell myself.

As I crunch out over the ice, cleats and sticks at the ready, I spook an Arctic fox, who dives away from me.

It's more than just cold. It's "take precautions so my eyelids don't ice shut" cold. And while it does worry me, the desolation and danger of this place, I have to confess that I'm also kind of thrilled.

See, this all lines up with my theory, too. Loki is associated with giants and the color blue for a reason — blue as in glacier ice, frozen and frosty.

I pause in my hike. Above me, the Aurora Borealis streams out in a ribbon of colorful light. Even as I watch, the beautiful light show shifts and grows, expanding out in gorgeous greens and blues and pinks.

Suddenly, it doesn't matter to me so much that I'm alone out here. Yes, it's dangerous. But right now? This beautiful natural wonder is all mine, only mine. I spin in a slow circle, the lights a glorious streak over the star-strewn sky.

And then I gasp. There it is — Ullereng Lagoon. Somehow still liquid, the small lake reflects the Aurora Borealis above, a perfect mirror image of the streaks of color. I'm on a soft snow pile above the lagoon, and bits of ice from my cleats fall, rolling down the slope toward the water. Although much of the island is flat, this part is not, the lagoon appearing to be a snow-encased pit with a pool of water at the bottom.

It's beautiful. It's that awe-inspiring, bone-deep beauty that will stay with me forever.

But if I don't get back inside the hut soon, I'm going to freeze to death.

I take a step back from the edge.

But there's no land beneath my feet.

I sink into uncharacteristically soft snow, my leg

wrenching around. As I scramble for traction, my body falls backwards — toward the slope.

Toward the lake.

I try to scream, but my throat closes with the cold snow that fills my mouth as I tumble down and down. I claw at the snow, but I can't slow my fall. My body flips back with a neck-snapping jerk, and I have one moment where my eyes are filled with the sky — the darkness lit by magical lights, the colors of the Aurora Borealis bleeding into my eyes, obscuring the stars — and then I'm plunged into the lake, cold, clear, icy water washing over my head.

The impossibly cold water seeps into my clothing, weighing me down. My joints seize, my body going into a state of shock from the extremes in the temperature change. I just need to get to the surface — I have to breathe. Breathe first, then make it back to the outpost. To warmth. To life.

But no matter how much I fight to swim, I sink down and down and down . . .

CHAPTER 4
LOKI

cannot sleep.

The castle is quiet, the party long died down. There is only the sound of distant murmuring — guards on patrol. They stand watch to keep at bay any of the creatures here, the wildcats and monstrous beasts that plague this icy utopia; but Fenrir is right. We have grown soft. It is *boring* here.

I feel his rightness through every part of me, though I'll be damned if I ever admit it to him.

I scrub a hand over my face and roll out of my bed. The window is open, showing the wide, glittering expanse of Jotunheim spread before me. There is the city that has built up around this fortress, and far beyond it, other civilizations are beginning. Our frost giant legacy, spreading far and wide, thriving.

What the fuck is wrong with me, that I could look at any of this and feel *empty?*

I grip the window ledge in hard, tense fingers. I will need to find some way to reconcile this gnawing. I cannot let these thoughts spread. Fenrir is a cancer, and I —

A bolt of lightning streaks through me. Stronger than the gnawing, more insistent than any instinct or worry.

This is an alarm.

One I set personally, a magic I wove centuries ago, *eons* ago.

It flares again. Persistent. A ringing in my head, and I stand there for a long moment, struck dumb with confusion.

The alarm means the border of Jotunheim has been breached.

But that is not *possible*. It can't be —

Fenrir.

Fury overtakes me, and for a brief moment, I am glad for it. Something to *do*, an enemy at which to direct my restlessness — for Fenrir is now an enemy, if he defied me and opened the portal.

I dress quickly, throwing on my warrior's uniform, the leather breastplate and tight leggings that hold sheaths for knives, my favored weapon. Then I am out the door. I consider alerting my guard, but I want Fenrir alone. The less his ideals and actions spread to my people, the better.

Only a handful of those closest to me know where the portal is, let alone that it is still possible to reopen it. We all came through it to flee here, but I shifted the break after the last was in so it was more hidden, protected.

Fenrir is one who knows its location. He was trusted. He does not know how to open it — none do, save for me — but that does not mean he hasn't figured out a way.

Betrayal is metallic, but fury burns stronger.

I race out of the castle and through the city gates, crossing the wide, wondrous landscape of Jotunheim's snow and ice in deliberate, smooth strides. My boots sink into snow up to my knees, fluffy blankets of fresh powder, but I do not slow; my breath puffs into the air, warm against it, and my bare arms do not feel the chill. None of us do — we thrive here, at home in this frozen realm, and so as I run, I am infused.

Hills pass under me until I reach an outcropping of rock that stretches over a pond. It is small, frozen solid, and kept sheltered under this rock so any passersby would see only jutting black stone and heaps of snow, not the icy water beneath.

I skid to a stop at its bank and do a quick sweep,

but Fenrir is nowhere in sight. The snow leading up to the pond is undisturbed, no tracks other than my own.

And against a boulder across the pond, the portal is unchanged.

It is naught but a thin line half my height, perpetual light that shifts and changes like the ripples of color that sometimes paint the night sky. It is not wider, nor open, and I sigh in relief.

One beat, I stay motionless, limbs poised against the snow.

Then my eyes snag on . . . on *something*.

Something lies on the far side of the pond, paces from the rip, just next to a section of the surface of the ice that has been broken through. Whatever broke it lies perfectly still, a small mass of darkness half covered in snow, half in the icy water.

In a few bounding leaps, I cross the pond, and kneel next to the form. My eyes dart around, waiting for Fenrir to stage his attack — it is what I would do. Lay a trap, distract and trick —

The form at my feet moans softly. Something chatters, like teeth.

I look down at it.

It's . . . *alive*.

I alone can create corporeal illusions that are felt and can be heard.

Confusion and shock make a sudden war in my chest as I bend closer. The late hour covers everything in darkness, but it is never truly dark here, not with the stars and the moon and the reflective snow.

So I have enough light to let my eyes adjust on this bundle.

It's human. A woman.

She chatters again, her whole body shaking in the beginning stages of hypothermia. The thick clothing she's wearing is soaked and freezing, ice crystals hanging from the tips of her dark hair, her lips so blue she might have frost giant blood if she wasn't slowly freezing to death.

That war of confusion and shock lasts for only a beat longer before my muscles move of their own accord.

I snatch the woman up and cradle her to me.

She's so small, thin and light enough that I can carry her easily in one arm.

The portal behind me is unmoved. It gives no answers, no explanation.

But she might.

I am off again, racing back across the tundra, package in tow.

———

A human broke through my portal.

Not Fenrir. Or, at least, I did not spot him — perhaps he dragged this hapless mortal through and meant to retrieve her himself. All the better that I have her with me, then. She will reveal the truth.

If she survives.

Fuck, she's shaking so much — and then, halfway to the castle, she stops moving entirely.

Fuck, fuck, *fuck*.

I push faster, faster, a blur of blue and leather and streaking white hair as I claw the remaining distance. What would normally take hours passes in a flash, until I slam into the nearest door to the castle and tear upwards, vaulting over the stairs, ignoring the startled looks of passing guards — what a story they will have; the wild king Loki tore through the castle on a rampage, a lumpy bundle of vibrant orange cloaks in his arms. I do not stop long enough for anyone to get a good look.

I make it back to my chamber and slam the door shut.

The fireplace is unlit, but I quickly stoke a flame to life, prodding it higher, brighter.

Then I sit next to the flames, as close as I dare, and place the woman in my lap.

She still is not moving. I do not think she's breathing.

Fuck, *fuck* —

I rapidly begin stripping off her wet clothes. Sopping, feather-lined things peel off, and when she is nude, I begin rubbing her limbs, working heat into her body.

"Come on," I growl at her. "Come *on*. Live, damn you!"

I scrub her body, stoke the fire hotter, scrub harder—

After too long, much too long, she makes a small, pained moan in her throat, and begins shuddering again.

Relief floods my chest, and I sink back, the woman going lax in my lap, where she curls into a ball, holding her newly found heat in as much as she can.

I have been operating on instinct and panic — but in this moment, she is alive and breathing, and I realize that I have a naked woman in my lap.

A naked *human* woman.

This is not at all where I thought my night would take me.

I gaze down at her, studying her more closely now.

She is not as small as she initially felt, with long, lean limbs that curl around her now. Her hair is dark and thick, tangled in wet curls, but I imagine it is luxurious when dry, and I have the sudden, unbidden image of what it must feel like to be gripped in a tight fist. Her body is mostly shielded from me in her current position, which is honestly all the better; I had forgotten how attractive mortal women were. Her skin is soft and rosy, and she smells of exertion, of some kind of delicate soap.

Against my better judgment, I know I am growing hard beneath her.

Thankfully she's still unconscious.

Trying not to disturb her too much, I reach behind to my bed and pull off one of the fur-lined blankets. But when I try to maneuver her off my lap and into the cocoon of the blanket, she reaches out and grabs my bicep in her soft, thin fingers, and I am stricken with watching the sight of her paleness against my blue skin.

She is stunning.

And I realize, suddenly, horrifically, that the gnawing in my chest is gone. That feeling of something coming. That worry of missing someone I did not know.

I know her now.

Somehow. Some way.

It's *her*.

And I do not even know who she is, nor how she

came to be in Jotunheim, nor what plot Fenrir has enacted by dragging her to us.

But I do not try to push her out of my lap again, and when she adjusts in sleep, burrowing her cheek against my chest, I allow her to get comfortable, then I drape the blanket over us both.

I will wait until she awakens.

And then?

CHAPTER 5
FAITH

come awake slowly, achingly. My muscles feel heavy, and even the small shift I make without opening my eyes feels like moving through water.

Water. Ice. Cold.

I curl tighter into myself as the memory washes over me. I fell into the lagoon. The icy water swallowed me. I sank, down, down, down.

Alone. On an abandoned, uninhabited island. In the arctic cold.

Am I dead?

I take a shaking breath in, hold it, let it out. Something . . . tightens around me. I still keep my eyes closed as I carefully *feel*, urging my skin to tell my brain where the fuck I am.

Because I'm not dead.

And . . .

I think I'm naked?

But warm.

And surrounded by something solid, but still . . . nice? My hands run over the warm thing holding me. It feels like . . . skin. Cool skin, but not cold.

My eyes fly open, and I'm assaulted by the color blue. Okay. Not skin. This looks like an arm holding me, a big arm, but . . . blue.

I sit up, looking around. And see the blue arm is attached to a blue man. A giant of a man, easily ten feet tall or more. He has shockingly bright white hair, with *horns* curling from his temple over his skull. He is sitting with me before a fire, a fur of some animal loosely around us. And I, apparently, have been tucked up in his arms.

Naked.

"Why am I naked?" The words slip out of my mouth before I can bite them back. I scramble away, but not very far — I just can't *think* wrapped up in a stranger's arms. A big white fur slips down over the man's lap, and as the cool air, drafty despite the raging fire, hits my bare skin, I feel a moment of regret for leaving all that warmth.

And the man — the impossibly large *blue* man with *horns* — speaks. "What did you say?"

I blink at him, both understanding and *not* understanding making me confused. I did understand his words. He did *not* speak English, though.

He spoke Old Norse. The language of the Vikings. The language of the gods.

I blink at him. This . . . it simply cannot be real. I must be in some comatose state brought on by hypothermia. He's a figment of my imagination — how else can I explain a blue man who's practically a giant? The fact that he speaks Old Norse just proves that this is coming from my head.

For a moment, my heart sinks. I studied enough medical journals to know that when the body is close to death from hypothermia, the brain will come up with hallucinations to make death easier. Dr. Phillips made me read study after study on this — the Dyatlov Pass, airplane crashes in the Alps, avalanche victims. She made sure I knew the threat of the dangers of coming to a place like Jan Mayen Island.

But yeah — me naked, and warm, and beside a very hot blue dude who speaks Old Norse? This comes straight out of some fantasies I didn't even know I had.

Okay. I try to wrap my head around this. I'm probably dying. But . . . death isn't as bad as I thought it would be? I mean, if a girl has to go, at least the Grim Reaper is hot and blue? And horny in the literal sense of horns sprouting from his head?

A manic giggle escapes my lips.

"Do you . . . do you understand me?" the blue man says. "You spoke before in a language that is foreign to me."

"I understand you," I say in Old Norse. "I . . . I am just unsure. Of where I am?"

The man's brow had been wrinkled in worry, but as soon as I respond to him in Old Norse, he seems relieved. "You are somewhere safe. Can you tell me how you got here, though?"

"I fell into a lake. Woke up here." I look down at myself. My nipples are tight — a result of being nude and the chilly draft in the air that exists despite the roaring fire. And between my legs . . . well, I'm hot there, and that's entirely a result of the man before me, his broad shoulders impossibly strong, his cut chin and sharp cheekbones, his eyes that seem almost silver.

"Why am I naked?" I ask again, this time in Old Norse.

"Because you were freezing. Who are you?" the blue man asks, peering down at me with the same intense curiosity I seem to have for him.

"I'm Faith Beck." I almost want to add my new title to my name — *Doctor* Faith Beck — but I can't think of the Old Norse for an academic. The Vikings didn't care too much about university education.

"I am Loki, King of Jotunheim," the blue man says, and that absolutely cinches it. I'm hallucinating. There's no way an enormous, hot man speaking Old Norse just happens to be Loki anywhere outside of my broken brain.

Huh. Okay.

Well.

I take another deep breath.

"I must confess, I am . . . concerned about your presence here," Loki says.

"Same."

"I feel it best to keep you hidden, here, in my chambers, until I determine how you broke through the portal."

My poor mind fritzes at this. Portals? Okay. Huh. Well, the salient point is that Loki wants to keep me in his room. My eyes drift to the bed behind him. Loki wants to keep me alone in his bedroom.

I have to give it to my pitiful cold brain — this is one hell of a good hallucination, in more ways than one.

"What do you mean?" I ask, leaning into the fantasy my body is so desperately trying to serve me. "Am I to be your plaything?"

Emotions flash over Loki's face, settling on a smirk that has me melting. "If you so wish," he says.

"If a girl's gotta be trapped with a Norse god, then . . ." I start.

"I am no god," Loki says. "I am the giant who fought the gods."

Semantics. "Giant?" I rake my eyes over his body. He's easily about ten feet tall, but we both know I'm not speaking about his height. "How giant are you *really*?"

If I thought the smirk on his face before was hot, the one he gives me now is positively scorching, and I feel it right between my legs. "You are a human who likes to play with fire," he says in a low growl.

"Better than playing with ice."

"Ah, you didn't like the cold out there," Loki says. "But there are other kinds of cold."

I cock my eyebrow at him, letting my eyes linger on his lap. He still has the fur spread over him, but the bulge under it is undeniable to either of us.

"Oh?" I ask, remembering both his cool skin, and legend that had him linked to the ice giants. There were so many theories back at the university about the mythos of the ice giants, mostly that they were a hyperbolic representation of a warring Viking tribe. But as Loki stands, there's no denying that he *is* a literal giant, far larger than any human man I've ever seen before.

A largeness that seems to translate . . . everywhere.

Languidly, Loki spreads the big white fur near the fire and motions for me to approach.

"I thought you were going to show me coldness, not more heat." Despite being naked, being this close to the fire makes me sweat.

"Come here, my plaything, and let me show you."

Plaything? I mean, part of me bucks at that label, but to be honest? This is all in my head anyway, I'm pretty sure, so apparently a kinky part of my brain wants to be an ice giant's plaything.

I take a moment to consider. Yup, that checks out.

His big hand presses my shoulder, coaxing me to a sitting position. "I have been bored without new toys," he murmurs. The fire is hot, but the fur is luxuriously soft, giving me the feeling of floating on a warm cloud.

And his touch?

It's like a cool breeze, featherlight on my skin. I moan, arching my back as he traces a delicate line from my shoulder over my taut breast, circling my nipple. His touch is deliciously cold — not enough to freeze, but like the cool touch of a window in winter.

It makes me feel alive.

The thought zips through my mind, making me

wonder if this *isn't* actually a dream or a hallucination. It *feels* real. But then Loki's hand spans over my belly, his fingers brushing the top of my mound.

My legs part — had I been standing, I would have collapsed — and he slides his finger along my slit. His cool skin is so . . .

My thoughts shatter as his cold touch meets my warm wet, slicking over my clitoris in a way that sends sensation ricocheting throughout my body.

"My toy enjoys being played with," Loki says, his voice gravelly.

"Yes," I gasp.

He kneels in front of me, watching with fascination. Slowly, so slowly, he raises his finger, shining with my essence, and flicks his tongue out, tasting me. He relishes the taste, biting his lip and raising his eyes to mine in a way that conveys just how much of a delicacy he finds me.

There's a sound in the back of his throat that is part purr, part growl, and he crouches in front of me, spreading my legs wide. He takes a moment to stare at my pussy as if it were a feast to be devoured, and then he dives down between my legs, his long, cold tongue probing me in a blinding, searing rush of pleasure that makes my body collapse on the fur.

Loki slides his hands over my hips, lifting me up as if I were a tankard to drink from, not once withdrawing his lips from my pussy. He makes that purring-growl sound again, and I can already feel an orgasm building inside me, the tight coil of desire bordering between pain and pleasure.

My hips buck, and my legs spasm instinctively. My heels feel something hard — his horns. Tentatively, I slip my feet into the curling horns on his head, giving me the leverage I need to press my pussy higher, right into his eager lips. With a feral growl, Loki more than rises to the challenge, grinding his tongue into my clit.

It hits me then. The idea slams into me, and it is undeniable.

This is all REAL.

Death fantasy, comatose dream, hallucination — no. No. This is real. Somehow this man is really here, and he is really fucking me with his mouth. I know it's real. I've never been eaten out this well before, not by anyone. My brain couldn't make this up.

This is real.

"Loki," I plead, panting, barely able to get the word out, "please, *please!*"

He doesn't answer, not with his voice. But his tongue glides up my cunny, swirling over my clit. I am lava, but he is cool, slick like glass, his tongue gliding over my most sensitive bundle of nerves. It makes me think of the glass dildo I had before I met

Daniel, the way I'd store it in the freezer. My body heat took the cooling sensation away too quickly, and I didn't even mind — much — when Daniel threw my toy out.

This, though? This is so much better. His tongue is the perfect temperature, ensuring that my focus is *right there*, wherever his tongue is, a pinpoint of pleasure. He laps at me with perfect pressure, sucking gently on my clit before probing his tongue against it, his mouth rocking into me.

And then one of his big hands glides from my hip to my pussy. As his tongue swirls over my clit, his big finger pushes into me, pressing into my inner walls, another cold touch that leaves me gasping for air.

His finger inside me, his tongue lapping my clit, he finds that spot that makes my whole body come apart. I scream — an honest-to-god *scream* — as wave after wave of pleasure rolls over my body, my warmth spilling over his cold, my entire body coiling around the type of earth-shattering pleasure I could never have imagined.

CHAPTER 6
LOKI

have all the idiocy of a youth in heat. It has been ages — decades — since I have found anything even remotely close to release like this, and I fully lose myself in the taste of this woman. My woman. *Faith*. She is succulent, and I am starving; each swipe of my tongue in her tender folds intoxicates me more than our strongest mead.

So I am consumed with her, and do not realize the ramifications of what I am doing to her beyond thinking, *I must make her shatter with pleasure. I must feel her come apart. I must make her scream.*

And then, *I am making her scream.*

And then, a shock of reality, *I have a screaming woman in my bedchamber.*

My door flies open not two seconds after Faith

first cries out her pleasure, and I am at once furious that she is being interrupted and livid at myself.

I disentangle her feet from my horns and launch up in one fluid motion, planting my limbs over her body, attempting to shield her from the duo of guards who race in, too fast for me to pull up an illusion.

I had intended to keep her secret, to shield knowledge of her presence here until I could investigate Fenrir. Faith does not seem aware of how she ended up here, or why; if Fenrir is behind it, I will find out.

But keeping the presence of a human woman in Jotunheim a secret falls apart as assuredly as Faith does beneath my tongue.

"My lord — " They stop, weapons out, eyes wide as they take in my hunched body and the smaller form of Faith beneath me, her shuddering breaths of pleasure abating as she twists and looks up through my arms.

"Oh my," she says in a still, soft voice — that is, remarkably, full of wonder and curiosity and not the least bit terrified. From her state, she is now in a room with three blue monsters — I know how most mortals viewed us. And yet, she merely meets my eyes and frowns, waiting for my lead.

"Get. Out." I tell my guards. Never have I spoken

with such depth of intent, every syllable hung with murder.

"Um — right, sir. Of course, sir." They back up, scrambling over themselves, but there is no stopping this.

The whole castle will know who I have in my bedchamber within the hour.

The whole of Jotunheim will know within a day.

Fuck.

The door closes behind them, and I sit back on my heels, my focus going intently to Faith.

She sits up, pulling the fur around her chest with one hand. With the other, she reaches out, and lays the tips of her fingers on my cheek.

"You're real," she whispers, and it's that same sense of awe and curiosity.

My brow dips. "You believed — " *Oh, shit.* "You believed this was a dream? I should have known. I would not have behaved so abruptly — "

Her fingers come down and press on my lips, silencing me. My chest kicks with offense — no one treats me as such here — and I know she sees the flare of action in my eyes, because she gives a sultry grin that immediately has my head tipping, my hard cock throbbing.

"My Faith," I grumble. "Now is not the time."

"Why? I'm still just delirious enough that this seems like a really good idea."

"Precisely why we will take this no further." I encircle her wrist and lower her hand, though inside, I am reeling. This woman wants me, even now, though I know it is in part due to what she said — she is in shock. She needs to be cared for, not taken advantage of.

"My domain will know of your presence here," I tell her. "I wished to keep you shielded from them until I could uncover more truth, but I am afraid things will happen very quickly now."

"Truth? I fell through a pond. I told you."

There are small stains of pink on her cheeks where she is flushed with warmth and pleasure. I reach up to tuck a lock of her hair behind her ear, letting the pad of my thumb trace one warm spot, reveling in the feel of life returning to her bones.

"You were not coerced into coming?" I ask. "You did not see a form — possibly one that looked similar to me — that lured you in?"

Faith shakes her head. "I was the only person on that island. I — " She squints, thinking, and I have a sudden, overwhelming urge to kiss the spot between her brows that furrows so intently. "I fell. I slipped, I think. Goddammit, that was dumb." She drops her head into her hands, and I feel the reality of what happened to her begin to blossom in her mind.

When my people crossed through to this plane, I left but a sliver of the portal remaining. Not a large enough rip for any of us to pass through, certainly not a large enough rip for Odin or the other gods to follow us; and I cloaked it well on the Earth side to hide it from any who sought us. It was merely a fail safe, should we need to access Earth again.

But either the rip was just wide enough to allow a mortal to pass through, or something larger — and more dangerous — is at play.

"Stay here." I rise, adjusting my leathers and willing my cock to soften. A tall order, with Faith's naked body still soft and supple and oh so pliant on my floor. "I must address my council. I will tell them you were an illusion. That is all they will think you are. I formed the illusion of a human woman — albeit one who sounds *very* realistic. Your presence here will be safe."

"Wait." Faith pushes to her feet, barely holding the fur around her.

One breast slips free, her tempting nipple soft now, and I bite my tongue, summoning remarkable strength not to suck it into my mouth. What spell has this woman cast on me? It is not possible she is a witch; I would sense her magic. And yet I am utterly captivated.

"Why can't they know I'm here?" she asks.

I blink at her. "Why can a society of frost giants not know a human woman has broken through the centuries-old protective charms that keep your world separate from ours? Aside from the panic that will ensue, I am not convinced that your presence here is entirely by accident."

Faith lifts her chin. "You think I *intended* to crash through a pond and nearly freeze to death?"

She is adorable when she is trying to lord power over me — even more so because she *does* have power over me, and I suspect she is figuring that out. "Not you, my Faith. I believe one of my court is to blame."

"Okay. Well. I'm not just going to hide under your bed until — what? You take me back to the portal and chuck me into a frozen pond, and I freeze to death on *that* side of it? If someone pulled me here, I want to know who, and why, and how I can get back without *dying*."

"You — " But words die as Faith drops the fur completely, and I am at an utter loss to argue with her glorious naked curves.

She shuffles across the room and toes her damp

clothes. Her jaw sets, brow furrowed again, before she reaches for the bedding spread on my mattress.

I grab her arm, seeing what she is about. "You seek clothes? I will have some provided."

"In time for your councilors, who are apparently learning of my presence like *right now*?"

"You will not meet with them. You will not leave this room."

I am not used to my decrees being dismissed, particularly so flippantly. Faith doesn't hesitate — she bats her hand and resumes trying to peel off a thinner blanket to wrap around her body.

"I'm going to meet with them. This concerns me — my *life* — so like hell am I going to stay cooped up *here*."

"Like . . . Hel?" I do not understand this idiom.

Faith gives me a flat stare, wrapped up in a thin blanket. "I wasn't serious when I said I'd be your plaything. I'm sobering up quite quickly now, actually. And if you try to keep me trapped in here, I'll—"

"You are not trapped, my Faith." She *is* sobering, and it terrifies me. For while I have been lucid all the while, she is only now realizing who I am, what this means, and I am gripped with terror that she will come to regret ever having let me touch her.

I cannot imagine being told I would no longer have access to that body, to her little cries of pleasure.

I had only just begun to show her what I can do for her, for us both.

"You are not my prisoner, but it is not safe for you out there, and putting you at risk I cannot abide. Not only do I have more questions than answers about the portal, but my people — " I pause, dread bucking in me. "They will not take kindly to your presence here."

"How on earth could *frost giants* be afraid of a *human*?"

"You misunderstand me — "

"I'm going to this goddamn frost giant meeting, Loki!" Faith stops, laughs at herself. "I cannot believe that sentence just came out of my mouth."

And she turns for the door.

"My Faith — " Oh, she is *stubborn*, this one. Were all humans like this? Most assuredly not. "Just . . . wait. You cannot parade around dressed in a bed sheet."

She stops, only because she must realize I am right.

I sigh and turn to a chest against a wall. A moment of rummaging, and I pull out an old tunic of mine, a pair of leg wrappings that can be fashioned to cover her feet. It will do for now.

I hand them to her. "If you are so insistent, here.

But I would feel better if you stayed in this room, so I can know you are safe."

"Nothing about my presence here is *safe*," she says.

She snatches the clothes and holds them to her chest. But she hesitates, her eyes darting around the chamber.

"You . . . are seeking a place to change?" I clarify.

She nods.

I stare at her.

"Are you now being serious?" I prod. I had only moments ago had my face in her sweet cunt.

Faith glares at me as though she can read my thoughts. And I cannot help it — I grin at her.

She curses me and drops the blanket.

————

I need not call an official meeting — I can hear my council loudly debating from their chamber before I even enter. Faith trails me, her wide eyes absorbing every sight we pass, that now familiar furrow between her brows telling me her mind is lost in thought. I cannot fathom why she finds this place wondrous and not terrifying — her bravery is awe-inspiring, and knowing she is not afraid is the only reason I am able to walk into that meeting chamber with my head high.

The moment my council notices my presence, they go silent. All six sets of eyes turn to me — Sigyn, of course; other advisors; and Fenrir.

It is him I lock all my focus on. Him I read like a stalker sensing his prey for weakness.

Without a word, I step to the side, revealing Faith to the room.

I stay next to and a little in front of her, ready to dive to her defense should any have the poor sense to go after her. But all the room goes rigid, and I sense panic and confusion from most; but Fenrir is all hunger.

His eyes widen, pupils dilating, lips parting in a snarl too reminiscent of a wolf. I think he would lick his incisors if he did not realize I am watching him, and when he does, his fascination changes to a spike of molten jealousy.

"Friends," I begin. "It seems Jotunheim has a . . . situation."

"A *situation*?" one councilor bellows.

That sets off the room again, voices overlapping in shouts.

I escort Faith inside, bending so my hand falls on the small of her back as guards shut the door behind us. We cross the room to my chair at the head of the table, and when I lower into it, I look around, realizing there is no place for her to sit.

I pull her into my lap.

Faith allows me to, but I feel her go stiff.

"Do you wish to stand?" I whisper into her ear.

She shakes her head. Her form is so small against mine, but there is such strength in her posture, her bearing, that even though she finds herself in a room of giants, she seems tall.

They are yelling amongst themselves still, standing over the table while Faith and I alone sit.

Fenrir watches us, three places down. He is studying her intensely, and I know he is using his magic on her, reading within her mind. The smile that curls over his face is sickening.

"Fenrir," I spit his name.

His eyes flash to mine and I glare at him with all the force of my position.

"*Mine*," I tell him.

Fenrir draws back. There is surprise on him.

Then rage.

Now Faith is afraid. I feel the tension in her muscles, hear it in her tight breaths. That will not do — where is the warrior who took no thought to defying the king of the frost giants? And it is these men she fears?

She is not wrong to fear them, and I hate that her instinct is not misplaced.

I rub my hand on the small of her back, kneading the muscles there, until I start to feel her relax.

"Sit," I command the room.

Silence spreads again. Chairs scrape the stone floor as my councilors obey.

"It would seem the portal that has kept Jotunheim safe is weakening," I begin. "Enough that a single mortal — " I emphasize that, that only *one* has gotten through. " — has entered our realm."

"We've had peace for centuries!" a councilor cries. "How has this happened? *Why* has this happened? The barrier has never shown signs of weakening before!"

"If a human can enter, who next?" another voice adds. "Gods? Odin himself?"

Faith looks at me questioningly. I do not know what part of this confuses her, but I stay focused on the men around me and the way I subtly rub her back.

"One human is nowhere near the threat of Odin," I say. "But I do fear the same, that this weakening could beget larger problems."

"Problems?" Fenrir laughs. "*Reward* is more like! This is a gift of the fates. Were we not just reminiscing on the days of old? And now, look — a mortal woman! One who more than embodies the prizes we used to take. Look at those breasts, that—"

Faith flinches, and my grip on her tightens.

"Careful, Fenrir."

He cuts a vicious grin. "Why? She isn't a guest here. She's as good as a prisoner. And you're keeping her to yourself. Taking all the spoils rather than spreading goodwill among your loyal people!"

"She is not a spoil of war. There has not *been* a war, Fenrir. The barrier is weakening. We will uncover why, and we will send her back through, *unharmed*. Life will return as it was for us all."

Fenrir does not back down. He is arched over the table, shoulders rigid, that hunger in his eyes almost mad.

"You would cast aside such a golden opportunity?" he hisses. "You grow weak and selfish. Prove your dedication to Jotunheim. Treat her as the prize she is."

Faith goes absolutely still in my lap.

She is wondering how I will respond. She doesn't know me; she doesn't know that I would rather slice off my arm than give in to Fenrir, and I feel a single, involuntary shudder of fear tremble up her body.

I lean forward, and without a flinch, without a single lift of my finger, Fenrir's throat rips open.

Blood splatters across the table, and my councilors gasp in horror. Fenrir himself sees first the blood pour, then reaches for the wound, mouth gaping, eyes wide and rolling with terror.

I allow this to go for a breath. Long enough that Fenrir feels the shock resonate and shake him out of his hunger.

Then I drop the illusion.

"Do not. Question. Me." I tell Fenrir, punctuating each word. "You forget who I am. You forget what I am fully capable of. But I am, even now, benevolent; I will remind you of my power, but in a far less barbaric way. You will go to the portal and inspect it for weaknesses. You, along with—" I eye Sigyn, who nods immediately; two other councilors agree with mere glances. "These three. The four of you will leave at once and investigate the state of our protective barrier."

"Yes, my king," Sigyn says and pushes to his feet. The two councilors follow him immediately.

Fenrir alone stays seated.

I want him *gone*. I want him out of my castle, this city, so long as Faith is here. I do not trust him to be in the same room as her.

Finally, Fenrir shoves to his feet. "Yes, my *king*," Fenrir snarls the final word. With one last look at Faith — I will tear his eyes from his head — Fenrir trails the other councilors from the room.

The rest eye me, then Faith.

"She will remain under my personal protection until we are able to safely transport her home," I tell them.

But it is a half truth.

I do not wish to send her home. I do not know how I will bear to let her slip back through that portal, *ever*, if it is proven safe. Even just having her with me, her solid strength in my lap, has me sitting taller than I have in years. I am centered, I am clear, and it is all due to *her*.

This woman I barely know.

This human who has upset my life in a matter of hours.

My remaining councilors bow their heads. "Of course. No one will challenge you for her."

"Fenrir was out of line," one adds. The rest hum their agreement.

Good.

I level glowers at them until they leave, scuttling from the room with looks of fearful obedience.

Faith wilts against me as they go. I might imagine the way she presses closer to me, relaxing into my chest; but I *know* I do not imagine the way she shifts on my lap, the growing smell of her arousal that I had not noticed had waned from the air. In my bedchamber, I had been delightfully consumed by the scent of her; it had faded as we spoke and came here. But now, I smell her again, a sweet perfume of her longing for me, and I am again bordering on a man undone.

I do not wait until my councilors fully leave. I have claimed this woman, and they will know it.

I nuzzle my face into Faith's hair, letting her hear the long, low growl that rumbles in my throat. "I can smell you, my Faith," I tell her. "What of this brush with death excites you?"

"Death?" She twists, putting her face so close, *so close* to mine. "I don't think I'll be at all close to death with you here, will I? That was kind of the point. You . . . claimed me."

"Yes," I say without pretense.

I watch her face, carefully, but she nods, and again she seems curious only, that furrowed brow set, thinking, thinking, *thinking*.

I put my lips to that spot and taste it, licking the salt and sweetness from her skin. I am growing heady on the power I claimed, and I have half a mind to take her on this table.

If she will have me. I must know what thoughts are rolling through her, if they in any way mirror the cacophony in my head.

"Tell me what is happening in that mind of yours," I command.

CHAPTER 7
FAITH

oes he have any idea how hot that question is? *Tell me what is happening in that mind of yours.* Nothing makes me wetter than a man who wants both my body and my brain. I'll be honest — I may have only had a taste of sex with Loki, but I could tell the physical side of whatever this is was hotter than hot. But the idea that he cares what I *think*?

I mean, *goddamn.*

"You want to know what's in my mind?" I ask, a grin curling over my teeth. I'm deeply aware that I'm still on his lap, and the longer I look at him, the more I can sense how aware he is of that fact, too.

"With a feral snarl like that, I want nothing else," Loki says.

"I am thinking about how I have spent nearly my

entire life studying nothing but you, and now here you are, ready to be . . . examined."

Loki's eyes widen. "It has been centuries since last I walked the mortal realm," he says.

I smirk. "Like the idea of being remembered?"

"I have clearly made a . . . lasting impression."

I can't help it; I laugh out loud. He has no idea what his legacy on Earth really is. Even people who have never read the *Prose Edda* know Loki's name.

I don't tell him that, though. I somehow don't think the *real* Loki — every ten-foot, blue-skinned, wild-eyed inch of him — is ready to hear of Marvel comics or sexy fanfics about himself. And now that I know he was — is — real, it casts the *Prose Edda* and the Snaptun Stone and all those other iterations of Loki into serious doubt. Sure, he's long been associated with the ice giants, and even the MCU gave Tom Hiddleston golden horns, but . . .

Nothing, *nothing* compares to the real thing.

"You know," Loki says, his voice low, "I have not cared about mortals in a long time. But seeing the way you look at me now makes me realize that I clearly had forgotten just how sweet it is to be worshipped."

I laugh again, a short bark of true humor that shocks the sultriness right out him. "Sorry," I say, sobering. "It's just — I didn't say I wanted to worship you."

He arches a brow. "Oh?"

I twist around so I'm not just sitting on his lap; I'm straddling him. "I said I wanted to *study* you."

"Study?"

"On a scientific level," I say, tightening my legs around his waist.

His cock twitches under me. "You do seem the studious sort."

"Indeed." I run my hand over his tunic-covered chest. "Perhaps you may allow me to examine you?"

"For science."

"Obviously."

He stretches back, leaning his heavy frame against the chair. "Feel free."

Here? The question flashes through my mind, but I don't speak it aloud. Of course, Loki is clearly the leader of Jotunheim, and even if some of his subjects, like Fenrir, don't want to snap to attention, Loki has the power to enforce his will. This place we're in now, it's not just a home, but a castle. I was out cold — literally — when he first brought me here, but I saw enough of it as we rushed through the halls toward the council room to know that this is a grander palace than any I'd seen before, much more than the mead halls that predominated Viking literature.

And he is the king of it all.

And he . . . somehow . . . wants me. It is literally beyond every dream I've ever had. And, well . . . who am I to question that?

I splay my hand along his arm, the striking colors of his rich blue skin against my pale white almost enough to make me really consider an actual analytical comparison. But when I shift again, I feel his hard cock straining against his leather pants.

"In my world," I say, "there are many legends of Loki, but few images." I can't think of a way to call Loki "camera-shy" in Old Norse, so I let the sentence stand.

"An advantage of shapeshifting illusions," he says. "I suspect there are many, many images of me. You simply cannot tell it's me."

So, the shapeshifting is real and not just a legend. That is . . . exciting. I got a glimpse of his magic when he made us all think that he had ripped out Fenrir's throat. I put that disturbing image out of my head and consider what possibilities exist for him to shapeshift in more . . . pleasing ways.

This deserves consideration.

"You are thinking again," Loki says, and even

though he sounds amused, his hard cock beneath my legs insists on attention.

"I am something of a scholar," I tell him, unable to put "doctor of archeology and literature" into Old Norse.

"A scholar of . . ."

"You."

He arches a brow.

"And if I am to complete my studies," I say, grinding down on his lap, wondering if it is possible for him to feel how wet and hot I am for him through the leathers we both wear, "I would like to get the *full* picture of what you really look like."

He already gave me permission, so I don't ask again. I tug at his leather pants, and even though they fit like a second skin, the drawstring parts easily. It is extraordinarily gratifying that these leather pants are made the traditional way — a long string to cinch together an early version of a fly. It's simple enough to pull the lace out and reveal the full length of him.

I suck in a breath through my teeth, my eyes growing wide.

It's . . . he's . . . *huge.* But also — I don't know, I'd been half afraid that him being a frost giant would make us incompatible in terms of sex, despite some of the legends that had the Norse pantheon mingling with humans.

Size aside, incompatibility is not going to be a problem.

His shaft is a deeper blue than the rest of his skin, the head already glistening with pre-cum that almost seems to sparkle, like the frost on an early morning.

"Is this the part of me you wished to study?" Loki asks in a rumbling voice. A sly smile indicates that he has thoroughly enjoyed my fascination.

I shrug as if I don't care. "A girl has to start somewhere."

He shakes with laughter deep in his chest, and it makes that enormous cock of his twitch in an utterly enthralling way. I watch it, enraptured, and when Loki sees my single-minded focus, he grows still. I feel him staring at me. My legs are splayed across his lap, but I cannot stop my hands as I reach for his exposed cock. The shaft is velvety soft, but still rock hard.

He sucks a breath through his teeth at my first tentative touch. The skin here is soft, warm and silky, despite being rock hard. I trail my fingers down his shaft, and his balls constrict in desire. Pre-cum glistens at his head.

"And what have you learned, scholar?" Loki asks, his voice strangled.

I don't answer. Instead, I lean down and glide my tongue along the tip of his penis, tasting him as he tasted me. His entire body tenses as my tongue swirls over his head. My mouth is hot, salivating with desire, but his cock is strangely cool, just like the rest of his skin. It doesn't burn like ice, but the feel of it is intoxicating.

Tentatively, I shift so that I kneel between his legs and pull his cock to me, better angling it so I can fit him in my mouth. He's so *big*, but I relax my throat, focus on the feel of it, cool and enticing. I put a hand on either of his legs, leveraging my body up so I can better take him in.

His leg muscles are so *tense*. Without releasing his cock from my mouth, I look up at him.

Loki is arched back in the chair, his hands bunched into fists, his jaw tight, clearly fighting with himself to remain in control. I flick my tongue, tasting his tip and the sweet, cool glistening cum, and he growls. An honest-to-god *growl* of desire. I hum with pleasure, sliding my mouth down over his cock, and his hands fly to my head, fingers bunching in my hair, his arms shaking with the control he must be exerting out of fear of hurting me.

I take my time sliding my tongue back up his cock. His whole body quakes with desire as I lean all the way up.

"Are you . . ." He gasps the words. "Are you done with your studies?"

"You passed the oral exam with flying colors," I mutter, sure he won't get the joke. Before he can respond, I grab the hem of the tunic he gave me and rip it off, my nipples going instantly hard in the cool air. He watches with hooded eyes as I slither out of the leggings and wriggle back up onto his lap.

I hover there, my pussy inches from his cock. His is certainly the largest I've ever seen in my life, much less experienced personally, but I'm dripping with desire, my body more than ready for the challenge. He eyes me but doesn't move, letting me do this at my pace.

With one hand on his cock and the other on his chest to steady myself, I rub his tip against my cunt. His eyelids flutter as he fights to keep from bucking into me. I ease his cock into my entrance. My heart is thundering — it's not just the anticipation of sex, the tight coil of desire that demands to be released — it's sex with *him*, with Loki, with a literal ice giant, and by all the gods I want it.

I slide his cock into me and take him all the way to the hilt.

My body is on fire, my juices dripping down his icy cock in the perfect union of hot and cold. I shudder at the sheer pleasure of having him inside me, and his hands fly to my hips, keeping me there, his cock pulsing with desire.

For me.

Desire for *me*.

He wants this as much as I do, I can tell. My inner walls clench around his cock, and his fingers dig into my hips, pressing me against him. He lets one hand slide down, one finger slide *in*, parting my folds and finding my clit. It's all pressure, all cold and hot, all hard and soft, and he rubs against my clit in a way that pushes my senses against his cock.

I gasp, almost unable to breathe from the sheer sensation of it all. He's *so* big; it should hurt — but it doesn't. He fills me up, and it feels so *good*.

I can't help the waves of pleasure that make my cunt practically vibrate, and he feels it all around his cock. With a feral noise in the back of his throat, Loki roars, standing up without removing me, holding me firmly against his cock. The chair he'd been sitting in clatters down as he slams me on the table. He keeps one hand on my hip to steady us and the other hand over my clit as he pounds into me.

I arch off the table to meet him, and it's the perfect angle. With a scream of pleasure, I climax.

I have never known such bliss.

CHAPTER 8
LOKI

This is the second time Faith has screamed her pleasure loud enough to rattle my castle's walls, and I know in that moment that it will not be the last.

I whip a glare to the door, but no guards charge in this time — indeed, the door is actually left *open*, but then Faith shudders beneath me, and I am too far gone to care.

This is my domain.

Fenrir is on his way out.

No one will disturb my taking of her, *no one*.

That she is so eager for my cock has me fighting release with every tremble of her cunt walls around me. This is a dream, surely — I will awaken in my bed, alone and frustrated. There is no reason why this mortal angel descended into my lap, let alone is willing to take me, every inch of me. It feels impossible that her small frame is capable, and yet she widens her legs, and I feel the head of my cock pressing against the top of her womb, twitching and shivering.

She looks up at me, eyes fogged with desire. "Fuck me, Loki," she demands, and I am her obedient servant.

I prop my hands beneath her ass to lift her, driving ever deeper, hitting an angle that has Faith pitching her head back, mewling to the empty room.

"Never have I felt such a tight, eager hole," I tell her, "so warm and gripping my cock perfectly. Look at how well you take me, my Faith — every bit of me, sheathed to the hilt."

I thrust in, lingering there, letting her feel all of me deep inside of her. I revel in the sensation as well, dizzy with the deliciousness of her warm, tight walls gripping me.

"And you react so *beautifully*," I say. She must know the importance of this moment to me; she must understand how I see her, how I feel her. "Your little moans, your crooning cries, the way your eyelids are half-closed and your arms splayed over your head, the globes of your breasts bouncing with my thrusts, fully given over to my ministrations with your small body. You have surrendered to me, have you, my Faith? Allowing me to worship you. Worship I will."

I pull back, thrusting still, and find her clit with the pad of my thumb. My other hand roams higher, taking one full breast in my palm and lightly rubbing the bud of her nipple until it grows even harder.

"Loki — " Her voice is breathy.

"That is how you best say my name, pet," I tell her. "Unwound. Near obliteration. Come apart around my cock again. *Now*, pet."

I push on her clit and rub in hard, determined circles as I pinch her readied nipple. Then I pulse into her, rapid fire thrusts that bang the head of my cock deep in her womb, my own pleasure building, *throbbing*, pain at the restraint making my jaw clench and every muscle in my body tense.

Faith's own body mirrors my tension. And as she begins trembling, the sensation I now know precedes her orgasm, her eyes flash open and find mine.

Then she comes with a quiver and a cry, and I fall apart deep within her, spurts of cum pounding into her walls as she vibrates and writhes and *screams*.

I dive down and plant my mouth on hers, swallowing her scream as my tongue dances with hers.

She tastes like a sunrise, like clouds parting on a gloomy day; she tastes like *home*.

———

"Does that satisfy your studies, my Faith?" I whisper into her ear as I lay over her, letting us both come down from the high.

"I . . . I'd say so, yeah," she gasps, and I am a man unraveled at the grate in her voice, utterly sated with pleasure.

"Truly?" I peel back to gaze down at her, letting my lips trail over her forehead, to her cheekbones, inhaling the scent of her, the delectable taste that is *her*. "There is no other question you have, no other test you would like to perform? I find that hard to believe."

"Oh. Yeah. I mean, of course; who knows how long until that portal will be deemed safe? I have loads of other . . . tests . . . I should perform."

Her mention of the portal seizes in my chest. But I lay my lips over hers and smile.

"First," I say, "allow me to broaden your research."

She makes a hum of confusion. "Broaden? You've fully *broadened* me already, I think."

She wiggles her ass, drawing my attention to my softening cock still in her pussy.

I grin and push up, guiding myself out of her and back into my leathers. As she sits up, I grab her tunic from the floor and pull it over her head, bending to rewrap the sad leggings that do very little to protect her tiny feet from the cold stone of my castle.

I will have proper clothes fashioned for her. Immediately.

She lets me dress her, a dreamy smile on her face, full of bliss and relaxation, her hair tousled from my thrusts on the table.

I gently tug her curls apart, and then I reach for a side table with some refreshments still for the councilors. As I hand her a mug of water and a small cake, she takes both so quickly that my chest seizes again.

"You are hungry," I guess.

"I didn't realize I was, but — " She swallows the cake in almost one bite. "This is really good.. Like, *really* good. What is that?"

"An apple fry bread. Come — I will have trays of it prepared for you."

The look Faith gives me is all sardonic. "I don't need *trays* of cakes, Loki."

"You enjoyed it, though. You will have as many as you desire. It is my renewed purpose in life to give you every pleasure."

Her lips part as though she will argue, but she must determine — correctly — that there is no winning this fight.

She sighs, studying me, but it is not her usual curiosity. It is . . . softer.

"I can't tell if you are serious or not," she says finally. "I'm as much of a fascination to you as you are to me, right? That's what this is."

Would it terrify her to know that since her arrival, I have felt a peace I had been lacking for years? Would she run screaming back to the portal should I tell her that she is the embodiment of desires I didn't even know I have?

I will tell her. Slowly.

I extend my hand to her. "Allow me to show you."

Another sigh, and she takes my hand as she scoots off the table. The moment she is standing, her eyes widen, and I see her legs tighten together.

"Is there a — um — room where I can clean myself?" Faith asks, her brows pinching.

I grin at her, absolutely feral. "No."

She blinks. ". . . no?"

"No." I tug her closer to me. "I claimed you, my Faith. This is what I demand in repayment: a mark of my hold over you."

Her eyes widen into perfect circles. Then a slow, small grin spreads across her face, her cheeks tinting the faintest, most gorgeous shade of pink.

"No one will *see* it — "

"No, but I will know my seed is still inside of you, dripping down your sweet legs. I will know, and all will see my obsession for you." I take her hand and lay it over my cock, already swelling for her again. "And later, I will spread you across my bed, and I will clean you myself. But for now, this is how I am marking you."

I am tempted — so tempted — to make good on that promise here, to spread her out and clean her with my tongue.

Faith gasps, winded, and barely seems able to nod. "Okay. Well. Wow. Okay. I mean, I guess we'll test the boundaries of my birth control shot against frost giant sperm, huh?"

"What?" Some of her arrangements of words are so foreign.

Faith bats her hand, searching for interpretation. "It's a method to prevent pregnancy."

"Ah." Again, I feel my chest sink, for reasons I do not dare admit to her.

"Come. There is much you must see," I tell her, and I guide her from the council room.

———

I take her to the central banquet chamber. It is midday now, empty save for a few servants straightening the room for tonight's dinner feast. The far doors are open wide, letting in whirls of snow flurries and the soft white light of a clear day.

Faith stops at the threshold, and the breath surges out of her again. I try to see this room as she does, for the first time.

It is a striking sight.

The ceiling towers tall, even by frost giant standards, all the walls done in deep, dark mahogany and oak, richest browns and reds. Rafters peak to hold the ceiling aloft, a few of them even now tangled with holly and ivy for pops of greenery. Roaring fires stay stoked at either end of the room, filling the space around the rows of tables with the intoxicating scent of woodsmoke and burning.

"This is like the best preserved historical site," Faith says, hands going to her mouth to suppress a hypnotic, childlike giggle.

I smile down at her. "Much of my court gathers here every night for a feast. We live simply, but peacefully."

"Peacefully," Faith echoes. "*Most* of you, you mean."

"Ah." I step closer to her. "Do not let Fenrir bother you. So long as I have claimed you, you are safe. Fenrir was a bad first introduction to frost giants. You will see at the feast tonight."

She whips a startled look up at me. "Oh, *yes*. Yes, I'd like to see that, please."

"I said you will see it."

"I know. I know. I'm just — this is *amazing*, Loki. I still can't really believe I'm here. *Here.* In a castle in Jotunheim. With . . . you."

"Well," I tuck a piece of hair behind her ear, "I am a master of illusion. Perhaps this is all an elaborate hoax I created to make you happy."

Faith rolls her eyes. "You're not *that* good."

"Ouch, my Faith, you wound my pride."

She playfully bumps her elbow into my side as she steps deeper into the banquet chamber, her eyes snatching to every detail. The milling servants glance at her, do double-takes — I see them whisper and eye me, too. There is unmasked fear on their faces, but none run screaming from the room. Likely news has spread already, preparing them that a human is here; likely further, news of my claim over Faith has spread as well.

Even so, that predatory sense of protection wells again, though I know no one else in Jotunheim would dare challenge me like Fenrir. With Faith, though, I am almost manic with needing to keep her safe.

My people are right to be afraid, though, that her presence here means we are at risk. I do not fault the averted gazes of these servants, nor their palpable hesitation. But they must see that I am unconcerned — mostly — so their own fear does not spiral. I will keep them calm and safe, as I have always done.

I wave over the closest servant, who gives Faith a wide berth where she is slowly, almost dreamlike, creeping towards the open doors.

"Find warmer temporary clothes for my guest," I say. "And bring a tray of apple cakes and other refreshments."

"Guest, my king?" the servant prods, brow furrowing in a shock of wonder.

"Yes. *My* guest."

The servant blinks quickly. "Yes, my king. Of course." He bows, his eyes darting to Faith once more, only in curiosity now more than fear, before he scurries off.

I trail Faith to the open doors. There, spread wide below the slight plateau on which the castle sits, is Jotunheim.

"Oh, wow," Faith exhales.

I smile at her exuberance. The city looks as it always does, dozens of huts and buildings scattered throughout meandering snowy streets. I can see movement from here, my frost giants going about their day in peace.

My chest swells for a moment, seeing Faith's joy, feeling that sense of peace.

This truly is paradise.

Now. With her.

"Loki," she whispers. "Can we go there? Can I see it?"

"Of course." I touch her arm, drawing her attention to me. "After you are properly attired. I sent a servant in search of better temporary clothing for you. I will not see you freeze to death after I worked so hard to save you already."

She rolls her eyes — I adore making her do that. "Fine. I guess that makes sense. I'm also — " Her gaze briefly drops to her legs, where I know my seed still stains her, and my grin deepens, darkens.

As though sensing we speak of such things, the servant returns with a bundle of clothing and a platter of food. His fear is still potent, and I note that the other servants in the hall are at the far edges now, going about tasks with shaking limbs and quick, bent whispers.

This will not do.

I motion for the servant to set his goods on the table. He obeys and hurries off.

Then I grab Faith under the arms and set her on the edge of the table as well.

"If you are uncomfortable," I say quickly into her

ear, the beat of her heart threatening to unravel me; but I will focus, I will maintain control, for her, "tell me so. But I am insatiable, my Faith, and I was not lying when I said I will see to it that everyone in Jotunheim knows you are mine."

"What — "

She gets no chance for a question as I push her flat on the table. I stay bent over her body, the chilly air billowing in from the open doors, but the heat of the fireplace wars with it so a series of goosebumps pops across her skin.

"You wish to see my kingdom? You will see it. After I have properly readied you."

"*Loki* — " It is half laugh, half gasp. "Here? With — "

Her eyes go to the servants. A stray guard walks the hall.

"They're afraid of me," she notes quickly.

"Yes. They need to be shown whose you are." I kiss her neck, trailing lower. "Do you allow me this, my Faith?"

I take a bite of food from the tray and hold it over her lips, a bit of simmered ox.

She props up onto her elbows, and her lips part for the bite. She is flushed, her breathing quickened, and she is quiet long enough that I wonder if this is pushing her too far.

But then she nods. "I guess we both get to eat," she says, chewing, then her eyes pinch at her own joke.

I smirk at her as I push her back down. "Indeed we do," I say, and I am nearly giddy. It has been too long already since I tasted her — and now that she is in no dreamlike fog, now that she is fully present and eager for me, it will be all the sweeter.

The servants and passing guards watch, and word will further spread. They will fear her and what she signifies, yes, but they will know that I have claimed her, and that their king is, as ever, in control.

I crouch beside the table, loop Faith's legs on either one of my horns, and delve my tongue into her folds.

CHAPTER 9
FAITH

Once we've both had our *fill*, I find my curiosity about Jotunheim is a little abated. It's hard to want to explore a city when your body is completely boneless in utter bliss.

So I don't protest when Loki lifts me up and literally carries me back to his chamber. I have had precious little time to actually rest, and, frankly, nearly dying and then discovering that not only is Loki real but entirely fuckable has made me ready to collapse. Loki sets me on a downy mattress, but it's not until the bed creaks as he slips in beside me, pulling me close, that I truly fall into a deep sleep.

When I wake up, there is still light outside. I'm not sure if it's because I've slept a full twenty-four hours or if we're actually in the Arctic when sunlit hours go on and on, or if Jotunheim operates on an entirely different plane of existence. I don't suppose it actually matters, though.

I stir from the bed, and Loki shoots up, concern etched on his face.

"You can sleep more," he says. "I should have been more aware of your needs."

He looks utterly anguished, every line in his face speaking tales of sorrow.

"Loki," I say, shoving the furs off me. "I'm *fine*. And I don't want to sleep more! I want to *see*."

"See? See what?"

I jump onto the floor, ignoring the cold. "Everything!" I am still clothed in Loki's old tunic, and without a belt it reaches past my knees. "I told you I'm a scholar. This? It's better than . . . anything," I finish lamely as Loki stretches and gets up from the bed.

I was about to say that it was better than any archeology dig, but that sounds grim, and I'm not sure how Loki would feel to know how consigned to history he's become. Forget what time of the day it is; I don't know what time of the *year* it is any more. I fell into a portal that leads to a different *realm* — who knows if time works entirely differently here! Maybe a decade has passed back home; maybe only a second.

The idea of the world moving on without me

makes my heart twinge. I have people I care about — my friends, mostly — and I don't want to just leave them with nothing but ice and a mystery in my place. But I push that thought from my mind as well, at least for now. I want to take advantage of my time here for as long as I can.

I became a scholar to learn. Daniel may have been a prestige-chaser, wanting to study history so he could somehow make it, but I only ever wanted to know things. History was a puzzle for me to figure out. I didn't have to make a once-in-a-lifetime discovery — although it certainly makes me happy to know that I have kicked Daniel's ass in that department.

Even so, I truly just want to *see* Jotunheim. I want to experience it. I want to know it.

"We must clothe you suitably," Loki says, oblivious to the giddy excitement the anticipation has made rise in my body. "Loathe as I am to dress you, it is colder in the city than I think you are accustomed to."

My gear is dry now, thanks to the warm fire in Loki's hearth. It's arctic-grade thermals, but it's also neon orange, and nothing will make me stand out more. Besides, Jotunheim is warmer than Jan Mayan island.

Loki is oblivious to my line of thought. "Here," he says, "the clothing my servant found."

Loki produces a dress for me, fine wool woven in tight stitches. A part of me wishes I could go to the looms and see how close our replicas of weaving from that time period are, but I settle for simply donning the white woolen smock and layering the gray-green apron woven with silver thread embroidery over it. I pull on three pairs of socks to make the slightly-too-large boots he hands me fit better. All in all, not bad, not bad at all.

Loki, however, is frowning.

"What's wrong?" I ask, worried that I look stupid. I have absolutely worn historical clothing before — re-enactments are part of the fun — but maybe I did something wrong?

"You should wear nothing but gowns of gold and precious gems," Loki says, his voice oddly serious.

I laugh, and his frown deepens. "I thought you preferred I wear nothing at all," I quip, and I'm relieved when his trademark smirk reappears on his face. "Come. I'm dying to see Jotunheim."

Briefly, his smile fades, and I think he's not sure if I'm serious or not. But I bound to the door, and he follows, catching up with me quickly.

He keeps looking at me with that same quirk on

his lips, as if he cannot quite figure me out. I suppose to him, this is regular, everyday life. But to me?

"What I love," I say, and *that* makes Loki lean in close, his attention rapt, "is the way Vikings congregate in small villages. Communities were family units."

"Of course," Loki says. "Is that not how humans live now?"

"Some do, I guess. But most of the people I know live in a huge city. I share a building with dozens of people, but I know hardly any of them by name."

Loki gapes at me. "Truly? How can you trust a neighbor you cannot name?"

"No one trusts anyone," I say. We lock our doors every night. We trust that people are too tired or constricted by laws or busy to commit crime.

For all that movies portray Vikings as violent, the truth was that they lived very peaceably among themselves. There was a central mead hall from which to rule and outlying houses for smaller families. Everyone took care of everyone else.

"I've always wanted to live in a place like this," I say as Loki leads me to a balcony overlooking Jotunheim.

"I don't understand the way your cities work," Loki says. "Why would you not at least populate your building with family instead of strangers?"

"I didn't have any," I say. "Not enough. My mother moved from — " I pause, thinking. How can I explain my mom moved from New Jersey to a Norse God who lived before America was colonized to include a New Jersey?

I try again. "My mother lived on the east coast of my homeland. My father lived in the desert lands to the west."

"Your homeland must be large." Loki's eyes grow distant. The Viking reputation for invasion happened because there was so little livable land in the icy fjords. As families grew, they had to invade the coastal regions to the west for fertile fields and spacious areas.

"America — that's my homeland — it is large," I say. "I was raised in the desert lands, away from my mother's family." I've met only a handful at an occasional holiday or funeral. It used to sadden me that I had dozens of cousins who were close to each other, but I could pass them on the street and not recognize them. I followed a few on social media, but it was clear from the start that we had little in common. They were deeply religious and intent on starting families; my values lay elsewhere.

"What of your brothers and sisters?" Loki asks.

I laugh. "None. My mother died when I was little, another reason why I don't know her family so well."

Loki's brow creases in a frown. Even though I speak lightly, he must know the pain in my soul to have no family left.

"My father had no siblings, the only child of only children who had him late in life, and they were gone before I was born. So it was just Dad and me in the desert for a long time. He got remarried when I was . . ." I glance at Loki, unable to find an adequate word in Old Norse for "high school." Sighing, I continue. "When I was older. He has a new little family with toddlers to take care of. He celebrated with me when I got accepted to a prestigious university, and he sends his love, but . . ."

Loki's face shows fury. "He should not dismiss his oldest child so quickly," he growls. "It is wrong. You need a family."

"I can take care of myself." My father and I have grown apart. My step-siblings are cute, but I hardly know them. He's my dad, but he's *their* dad primarily.

So, the Study Group became my home. My family. My community. And it's not the same, but I do love them.

"A family is not there merely for survival," Loki protests. "A family is needed for — " He sputters, unable to complete the sentiment. Instead, he sweeps his hand out toward Jotunheim.

I'd been so wrapped up in the story of my past that I hadn't had a chance to really look at the Viking land I was so keen to discover. I look now.

Loki's palace obviously serves the place of the mead hall in the community. It's in the center, built on a hill, with all the rest of Jotunheim spilling out underneath it. I cannot help but analyze the layout. Jotunheim shows signs of being planned, but also signs of chaotic growth — the grid of the streets quickly falls away.

"This is the oldest building," I say, glancing at Loki and awaiting his nod of confirmation. The palace had been constructed first. "And then — " I gesture to the nearest buildings — stables and barns, some areas that are obviously used for storage, open buildings where I can see men and women weaving, cooking, baking, doing carpentry, smithing, and other crafts. All the people I can see from here look generally happy, chatting away, laughter bubbling up.

"For a century, everyone lived here, in the palace," Loki says. "We grew to meet our needs, but my people did not start to spread out until . . ."

"Until you knew it was safe." That was how it was in the villages I'd studied on digs — areas with lots of violence and war were tight, contained, and protected. But when the village found peace and prosperity, it spread out.

"The gods could not pursue us through the portal I made," Loki says, looking out at Jotunheim. "But I have never forgotten their vengefulness. My people are always waiting for them."

He leads me from the balcony to some wide steps that spill out of the castle. As we descend into the main settlement, where the majority work and live, I crane my neck, trying to see as much as possible.

"What are you most curious about?" Loki asks.

I take a deep breath. "I can already tell that my thesis paper on how men and women shared house-hold duties somewhat equally in peaceful villages is proven true here; that gendered bullshit that supports the patriarchy can die in a fire." Loki raises an eyebrow; oops, I'd slipped into English. I switch back to Old Norse. "I think I'd like to see the spin-ning and weaving processes," I say. The actual construction of clothing was oft-debated — we have to some extent pieces of cloth that survived, but precious little. "But also the way you cook." I remem-bered the delectable bites of lunch I had. "All the tools. Everything! I'm just so — so curious! I want to know how things work; I want to see how you all live."

"Come," Loki says, laughing.

He leads me to the first crafting area, an open courtyard set up with looms. The sheep bleating nearby must be where the wool comes from. The happy chattering among the men and women as they dart bobbins through thread stops, however, as Loki comes closer.

At first I think it's because their king approaches.

But their eyes all land on me.

The castle was a little different. There were servants and guards and others who seemed — perhaps curious, but at least willing to turn a blind eye from me. I've gotten so used to Loki that I had not really stopped to consider our differences.

I'm short.

I'm pale tan, not blue.

I'm . . . human.

And the frost giants?

Not all of them look at me with the same eager eyes that Loki has.

He can tell, too. His jaw tightens, and when I move closer to him, he shifts his body protectively.

"My king," one of the women says, standing and bowing at him. Her eyes slide to me, disgust and fear and something else all evident on her face. Without another word, she turns and strides away, her steps just shy of running. The other weavers quickly follow.

"They are unaccustomed to humans," Loki tells me, his voice so gentle that I could cry.

Jotunheim is an utter utopia, paradise not only for the people who live in peace here, but everything I have ever dreamed of.

And while I have barely seen it, I can already tell:

I do not belong.

CHAPTER 10
LOKI

My people are right to be afraid. Faith's presence here means the portal is in question; their fear is valid.

I repeat that to myself as some leave their looms with scowls and blazing eyes.

I repeat that to myself as my fists tighten, muscles clenching, and I am ripped in two — my people have long been the sole source of my focus and concern, but now their attitude and needs threaten Faith. I cannot choose her over them, and I cannot choose them over her.

I do not need to.

My arm snakes around Faith's waist, and I draw her closer to me. "This is Faith," I tell the frost giants at the looms. Even those who are in the process of leaving the courtyard pause at my booming voice; I mean for it to carry. I mean to draw all attention, for command to be hidden in my easy words. "She is my guest and will be treated as such. There is no need to fear her; I have claimed her, and I alone hold the responsibility for her presence here."

One woman stands from her loom. "The portal?"

Others have gathered by now. Some are on the street behind us, pausing in their journeys; some peek in from beyond the courtyard, the barns and other outbuildings.

I have let rumors swirl this day. Now I will speak plainly.

"It is being handled," I tell them. "We all know well that magic comes with no small risk of unpredictability. Faith is a product of that. The portal chose to bring her here for reasons we are still investigating."

"The portal stands?" a man asks. "It hasn't broken?"

"Of course not," I say, and it is only a half-truth. It will not break. Not while I draw breath. "Faith's presence here is an act of fate. The power that keeps our world separate from hers appears to have selected her to be among us. You will find, as I have, that she is, at heart, Jotun. Faith has as much to fear of us as you do of her, and yet she insisted on coming out of the castle in good faith to learn our ways and partake of our customs. Her presence here is shocking, yes, but I think you will come to see her as a blessing." I pause. "If you give her a chance."

The last part rumbles out of me with all the force of my centuries of power. It is an order, not a suggestion, and I see my people resonate in that command. My words have affected them, and I am asserting control of this volatile situation as I ever have by telling them what to do in times of uncertainty.

A few nod. They trust me. I have earned it.

Others eye Faith still, stricken. It will take more than one speech to win them over.

But I will see to it that they will come around.

"Now, Faith." I look down at her. Her eyes are all liquid as she gazes up at me, and I cannot tell which part of my speech has touched her so. I lay my hand on her cheek. "What do you wish to know of our weavers?"

"I — " She swallows, righting herself, gathering back into her air of study and questioning. "I would like to see the processes."

"Which one?" asks a woman holding a basket of yarn. I know her — Tove. She oversees the weavers, has for decades.

There is doubt in her voice, that this troublesome mortal would care or know the right questions to ask.

"All of it." Faith turns to her. "Shearing to processing the wool to weaving the different types of — oh, and dyeing!"

Faith nearly *leaps* across the courtyard to Tove's basket of yarn. At the top is a bundle of the brightest red-purple, and Faith points at it in reverence.

"How did you get that color?" she asks, all wonder. "Usually it comes from a type of bug native to cactus plants, but I can't imagine you have any of those here, do you?"

Tove blinks at her. Then shoots a questioning look to me.

I nod, prodding her along, barely breathing. We are still watched by people on the road behind me; I feel eyes fixed, breaths held.

"It is a similar type of beetle, yes," Tove answers Faith.

"Still a type of cochineal bug?" Faith asks. "But indigenous to cold climates? Fascinating!"

Tove's face shifts. Disdain to confusion to . . . awe. "How do you know this?"

Faith smiles. "I've spent my life studying your king," she says with a glance at me. Her smile widens, and I can only return it. "And by extension, your ways." She looks back at Tove. "I am honored to be here. Truly. Thank you for even taking this time."

Faith bows her head and walks back towards me.

The tension I still hold does not abate, every muscle wound, ready to spring to intervene. As Faith comes back to me, I see the people of the looms resume their work, their hesitation now blossoming into the same sort of awe on Tove's face.

"Human," Tove calls. I must glare at her, for Tove quickly corrects with, "Faith, I mean. Come."

Faith stops, halfway to me, her eyes catching mine in a flash of wide awe. "Come?"

"Yes. Come. Or did you see all you wanted in one bundle of yarn?"

Faith whirls around. "No, of course not! Please, I'd love to see anything you — "

"This way." Tove sets down the basket and nods toward a building off of the courtyard where I know we store our dyes and fresh wool.

Faith doesn't look back at me as Tove leads her in, and I stay outside for a moment only, long enough to see Faith's back through the door as she exclaims, "Oh, this is *lovely* — "

There is a small chuckle behind me.

I turn to see a man smiling at the door, a basket slung in his arms. A woman near him smiles as well.

All around me now, smiles are beginning. They

are in disbelief, and most of my giants continue about their day, shaking their heads and laughing to neighbors about the curious human their king found.

But their fear is fading, and fading fast.

Here I had wanted to keep Faith locked away in my chamber, hidden and out of sight. But one moment in the village, and she is winning them over already.

I smile to myself and follow my Faith into the storage building.

———

I had come to take for granted my home.

All those thoughts I'd had of stagnation, of waiting for *something,* of even the same boredom that plagued Fenrir — I was a fool to tolerate them for even one moment.

Because through Faith's eyes, I see my home anew.

Every building we pass is a work of art to her. She studies the ornamentation along doorways, the carved scenes of patterned lines or mistletoe or beasts, exclaiming over the craftsmanship and atten-tion to detail.

Every group of frost giants we pass is fascinating to her, no matter what seemingly mundane tasks they perform. Preparing meals over a fire, mending a hole in a dress, sharpening hunting weapons in a forge — she spends long moments in silence simply watching each thing, her eyes nearly unblinking, utterly enraptured.

Fear and hesitation follow her through the village, but she wins over all we encounter with her natural charm and curiosity. Hers is not merely a fascination come from the foreign — she *knows* these things. She recites the processes we use for forging our weapons. She explains to me the shifting divide of village responsibility. She tells me the reason mistletoe is featured so prominently in our carvings and designs, and I am stunned in admiration.

"The gods were constantly trying to make themselves impenetrable," she says, tracing the outline of a carved bloom on the side of the schoolhouse. "When the goddess Frigg gave birth to Baldur, she was set on him being *the* epitome of their might, and arranged deals with all the elements so they would not harm her son. Baldur was impervious to stone, fire, water, and plants of the ground — but — " She eyes me, and a wicked grin spreads across her face, one that has me stepping closer to her with a matching, feral grin. "But you figured out the loophole. With mistletoe."

"Aye. It is not a plant of the ground — it grows

out of a tree's branches." I watch her fingers move over the carving, but the memory of this story has my heart slowing. "I killed him with a spear made of mistletoe. It allowed my people a chance to escape. He had ravaged our last village — he and his family used my people's bodies as the basis of their magics, creating forests from our corpses." My chest pinches. "There were so few of us left."

Movement pulls me, and I see the bustling street we are on, the milling frost giants, the *children* too, proof that we won even in the face of the gods and their constant search for ways to use us as fodder.

"It's so curious," says Faith, her voice soft to match my tone. "These were always just stories in my world. But you *lived* these things. They made you who you are now."

"Is that how you know so much about me?" I meet her eyes and smile again. "Stories told over roaring fires, tales of the might of Loki of Jotunheim—"

Faith laughs. I could hear nothing but that sound the rest of my days, and I would be content.

"Not quite," she says. "There are few stories told over roaring fires in my world now."

"How else has it changed?" I take her arm and begin guiding her back through the village. The day is fast closing — the evening feast will be upon us soon, and I have plans for my Faith before it. She has begun to put all fear of her arrival to rest among my people, but tonight will be a formal presentation of her to Jotunheim.

A formal presentation of her as *mine*.

"Honestly?" Faith leans into me. "You wouldn't recognize it. Much of the . . . *old ways*, as they're called, have been forgotten. They really are just stories in books. There are a lot of good developments — I mean, chocolate alone is to *die* for — but overall . . . there are a lot of things that we've created to do work for us now. Like clothing, for instance — there are whole machines that create fabrics now. No looms needed."

My eyebrows go up. "That sounds most convenient."

"It is. And it isn't. The quality has been completely lost, and most of the garments made end up in awful landfills — shit, I'm sounding so morose. It really isn't that bad." But Faith squints, and she sounds more like she's trying to convince *herself* rather than me.

"What of the — " My mouth goes dry. " — the gods? Have they led these changes?"

Faith blinks up at me as we make the final turn onto the main palace thoroughfare. "The gods? Oh,

Odin? No. They haven't been worshiped in centuries. They're as much stories as you are."

I come to a full stop, Faith on my arm. "What?"

She tips her head, trying to gauge my reaction for happiness or fear — honestly, my body is humming with a mix of both. "There are some who still worship them, of course, but they are very, very few. The Norse gods are mainly myths at this point."

"They do not threaten those who disagree with them? They do not hold relentless sway over the world?"

"No. Mortals do that well enough ourselves."

Odin and his gods no longer rule Earth. Our greatest enemy has been reduced to myth.

I laugh. It shakes through my body, a laugh of such relief from tension I have been holding for decades. Centuries. *Lifetimes.*

I lift Faith into an embrace and kiss her fully, tasting her sweet mouth as soft flakes of snow begin falling around us.

"This is the best news I have had in a millennia," I say into her.

Faith locks her arms around my neck. "I wish I could have brought it to you sooner." She pulls back to look at me and runs a finger down my cheek. I feel the tension in it releasing, muscles I'd long held in a position of readiness now coming undone. "Have you lived in fear of them all this time?"

"Yes," I say immediately.

She leans in to hug me. Though I am holding her, it feels, suddenly, as though she is holding me.

"If the gods are no longer threats in your world," I say into the curve of her neck, "then perhaps it will not be so dangerous to have the portal open on occasion."

Faith goes stiff against me. "Oh?"

"Perhaps," I echo.

She could visit me in Jotunheim. I could visit her on Earth.

It is too big a dream to consider.

I have devoted my life to protecting my people — the thought that we do not have to live in fear is freeing, and terrifying, and *massive*.

Could we lower our guard? Could a few of us travel back to Earth and figure out where the gods went, and determine once and for all if they are still a threat on that planet?

Should we go back? Earth was our home once — but that was so long ago that most no longer remember it. *This* is our home now, and it is peaceful and safe and gives us everything we want.

I set Faith back on the road and smooth her hair over her shoulder.

"That means you are free to return home," I say. "Once my party comes back with news about the tear. We will test it, of course. But if it is safe, then there is no reason why you should not be able to go home."

I am gutted saying this to her. My tone is hardened steel, fury licking at the edges of each word, and I know Faith hears it.

She slides her hand around my arm again. "That's . . . good news," she says.

Does she sound hesitant?

I dare not hope. Too much goodness has come from her arrival already — I cannot tempt fate with hoping that she would, in any impossibility, choose not to go home.

That she would choose to stay with me.

"Come," I tell her. "The feast will begin shortly, and you are long due for proper pampering, my Faith."

She looks up at me with a sudden burst of bright eyes. "Oh?"

I sigh, adding a flare of melodrama. "No matter how delectable your scent, I cannot be so selfish as to parade you around the evening's meal disheveled from our lovemaking. You deserve gold and jewels, my Faith; I was serious about that."

She smiles, and the world is right again. "Well. I'm not going to argue with *pampering*."

"It is not entirely selfless on my part. I crave knowing how you will look properly attired. Specifically so I can then peel that attire off your body later."

She giggles and pushes into me, and I absorb her happiness like the sun after a long, brutal storm.

CHAPTER 11
FAITH

Back inside the castle, Loki walks with purpose. The halls are so large and long that they create a dizzying maze, but everyone we see seems more than eager to jump to attention and offer any aid. *They don't all hate me,* I think, recalling the weaver I had met when I first left the castle walls. *Maybe they could come to accept me.*

And then I remember Loki's words, about how I will have to leave.

I take a deep breath and let it out in a shuddering release. I will have to enjoy what time I have.

Every dream dies at dawn.

I will live in this one as long as possible.

Knowing my time is limited makes every observation more dear. I make a point to look into each face we pass, to smile, to pretend, at least for a bit, that I belong.

And to my surprise, they smile back. It's more than just servants being polite or doing their job. "They seem . . . happy?" I mutter as we pass a pair of men who bend their heads respectfully, brandishing huge grins when I look back at them.

The corner of Loki's lips twitches up, and it's such a decidedly pleased look that my knees wobble, remembering the feel of those lips all over me. "They *are* happy," he says as if only just now realizing the truth. He glances down at me. "They are happy because I am happy."

This is more than just the mead hall allegories I'd read about in *Beowulf*; there is genuine joy on the faces we pass. I wonder if this is a reflection on the legends, that if the king is pleased, his people are as well. Perhaps that old adage comes from an actual mythological source, and Loki's joy seeps into the roots of Jotunheim.

And then I remember Fenrir, the displeased councilman who had to be threatened to obey. The weaver who tried to leave rather than be near me. No, Loki's people aren't on some magical pipeline to his bliss; they just like him. As a king and a person. And the obvious joy painted on his face reflects in their own, the same way I felt joy when Cassie, a girl from my study group, got accepted into the Egyptology program at Cairo last year, or the way Elanor passed her Master's thesis for her study on Merlin.

Honestly? That's such a huge turn-on, and I didn't even know it. Academia can be so fucking cut-throat, and the way the girls celebrated each other's wins was a rarity. Daniel had his own sort of study group, and they were a bunch of assholes, always looking for a way to undercut one another, always hoping that one person's success would lead to a leg-up for their own success, but more hoping for each other's failures so they could seize unearned opportunities.

I suppose Loki's been king of the frost giants for so long that everyone's settled into their roles. It's a community more than a monarchy, despite the fact that there is a clear leader.

If there's one thing I'd learned from my Viking studies, it was that challenges to a good ruler were rare. The only time someone issued a challenge in the mead hall was because the ruler was inept, unfair, or incapable of protecting his people. Loki's been king since Odin ruled the Norselands, and it's clear that he's stayed in power because he's *good*. The relief and happiness on the faces of the people we pass are joy both for him and because of him, and that's . . . that's astounding.

I watch Loki's ass as he strides a little in front of me, leading the way around a corner. Okay, maybe this bliss isn't the same as an academic accomplishment. Maybe I've gotten to the point of wanting to know him on a biblical level even more than an academic one.

I'm still willing to bet my study group girls would be abso-fucking-lutely cheering me on for this particular study of mine.

I'm so concentrated on what I see before me that I almost bump into Loki when he stops. He looks down at me, a smirk on that smart-ass delicious mouth of his.

Loki gestures for me to go into the room first. There are others inside — a tailor, I think, and some helpers — but one word from Loki makes them bow respectfully out. They leave behind various articles of clothing hanging from pegs, draped over chairs, and molded to dressing figures carved of wood and surprisingly modern. The clothes all look generally my size, and I'm touched by the effort. He must have arranged this while I slept.

The people scurry out of the room — an odd motion for giants — but they do not look displeased. Rather, they exchange knowing looks, no doubt well aware of the true rumors spreading throughout the castle.

Once the door closes and we are alone, Loki looks at me with a leer. "Undress," he commands.

"Why did you make everyone leave? I thought you didn't mind an audience." I ignore him, looking over the dresses and tunics prepared for me. Part of my mind cannot help but appreciate the craftsmanship. It's a fine weave on a wool soft as silk, made with more embellishments than I would have expected.

"I do not mind the entirety of all nine realms knowing that I make you mew with pleasure and scream with need using nothing more than my touch," Loki says, entirely too self-satisfied. "But I find that I prefer others to see you nude only while I am in the process of claiming you. Undress."

I cock my head at him. I shouldn't be surprised that a literal god and king of the frost giants is a bit bossy, but still. I remember the Snaptun Stone, the lips sewn shut on the only credible contemporary image of Loki that remains. The stone with its sharp chin and silly little mustache looks nothing like the muscle-bound towering blue-skinned god before me, but at the same time, I can't help but remember just how many of the legends had Loki wind up bound or gagged.

Loki leans down, so close that I can smell my scent lingering on him. "What has caused that impish smile?" he says, his voice low, almost a purr. There's a gleam in his eye, curiosity and a challenge.

I take a step back, my hand trailing over a belt draped beside a tunic. The supple leather is soft but strong, and I pick it up, winding it around my hands. "I was just thinking . . ." I say slowly, considering the gambit I'm about to play.

"Yes?"

"You've claimed me," I say. "But how can I claim you?"

A pale white eyebrow lifts as Loki contemplates me. But he doesn't protest as I step closer, the belt in my hand. I may have gotten the idea for this from the legends that had Loki bound by a giant snake or gagged to stop him from speaking lies and illusions, but Loki was also known in mythology for causing earthquakes, and so far the closest that's been true is in the earth-shattering climaxes he draws from my cunt. Maybe I can twist those bondage legends into something a little more fun, too.

Loki eyes the belt in my hand. "What do you have in mind?"

Oh, he's willing to play. Excellent.

"You're king," I say, walking around him in a circle. "And you're very used to having exactly what you want."

His eyes are like mercury, dark and dangerous. "Indeed." The word is both a promise and a purr.

I stand behind him, reaching for one of his hands, trailing my finger down his forearm before winding one end of the belt around his wrist. "I think you deserve a turn at being the plaything," I say. I reach for his other arm, and he willingly lets me put it behind his back, binding his wrists with the belt.

I move in front of him. "I think a king especially would appreciate a little . . . shift in power."

He arches an eyebrow again, but he doesn't protest. From the gleam in his eye, I get the distinct impression that this is *exactly* the kind of thing he's into. He just may never have gotten the chance to explore this kind of fun, given his position and how everyone in the entire land looks at him as the supreme ruler and literal savior of their people.

I lean in close. "Safe word is ormr," I say, picking the Old Norse word for serpent, since the legends of Loki bound by serpents initially gave me the idea to play like this. "You say that word, and everything stops, okay?"

He nods, the muscles in his jaw working. I glance down, unable to even pretend that I don't see the enormous hard-on he has at the mere idea of me playing with him. "Oh, you're eager," I say, salivating. I reach up, tugging at the laces of his leather pants, pulling them down and watching eagerly as his cock springs free. A drip of glistening liquid sparkles at the tip of his penis, and without thinking about it, I lean down and lap it up.

A burst of cool, salty-sweet floods my tongue. It's not hot like cum; it's delightfully chilled, practically refreshing. I almost laugh at my thoughts — but instead I part my lips and suck him fully to the back of my throat, humming, my tongue sliding up and down the long, hard length of his cock.

Loki groans, and his body twitches as he tries to pull from the meager leather bonds around his wrist. I can tell he's holding back; he could break the belt if he really tried, just as he could say "ormr" and it would all stop.

He likes this — not just what I'm doing to him, but being bound.

I pull back, using my teeth to gently scrape his shaft, not enough to hurt, just enough to remind him of how I'm in control. His balls twitch with desire, and I can't help donning a smirk.

"Sit," I order, my voice full of authority.

And Loki, king of the frost giants, bane of the gods, powerful and wise, sits at my command. He sprawls out gracefully despite his bound wrists, legs splayed on the floor, his shoulders back as he supports his weight with his hands behind him.

"You told me to undress," I say conversationally. "I choose to do so now. Not because you told me to. But because I want you to watch."

And with his eyes on me, I put on a show. I slither out of the dress, tossing it aside. His pupils dilate, his nostrils flaring, and I'm reminded of the way he said he could smell my desire for him. In the chilly air, my nipples are hard, and I let my fingers rove over my body, keenly aware of the feral way he watches me, like a wolf stalking prey.

Except I'm the wolf.

I'm in control now.

All he gets to do is watch as I twist my own nipples, gasping, closing my eyes at the pleasure of it. My hands explore my body, and I dip a finger into my folds, feeling the way I drip with desire for him.

When I open my eyes, I see him watching me. His chest heaves, and veins pop along his neck, his entire body tense. He wants nothing more than to snap the leather belt and pounce on me, I can tell.

"Good boy," I purr. "You play this game well."

He bites his lower lip, sharp teeth threatening to break skin.

"That deserves a reward," I say.

I stroll closer to him as casually as I can play it, but it's obvious that my body is responding to his, that I ache with need for him the way he does for me.

Loki closes his legs as I spread mine over his thighs. His hard cock juts up, dripping, and its cool temperature is the perfect balm to my hot cunt.

I don't drive him into me, much as I want it. Instead, I glide my pussy along the tip of his cock, playing with his head. I look up at Loki. His jaw is hard, teeth clenched, as he fights the impulse to push his hips up and pierce me with his cock.

"You have to wait," I say, looking up at him.

A growl rumbles deep in his throat. I realize that this is the longest he's gone without talking to me. It's like he doesn't want to risk saying our safe word so much that he dares not say a single thing.

I can feel his wide head pushing right at the entrance of me. Cool like a crisp winter morning, the sensation of it in contrast to my hot pussy is enough to make me want to plunge down. My walls seize with desire, wanting to pull his dick into me.

I shift so that his cock is no longer notched in position, sliding a little so the head brushes against my clit.

That gives me an idea.

I scoot down a little so my legs are wide and splayed over his lap, his hard-on inches from my open pussy. Loki shifts, bringing his knees up so my back can rest on him. I wiggle down, settling in his lap, my hips thrust up toward him. He looks down his broad chest at me, dripping over his legs.

I slide a hand gently over his pulsing cock, and more pre-cum spurts from the tip. He makes a moaning sound, needy and throaty, but he keeps his lips closed.

My cunt is close enough to his cock that he must feel the heat radiating off it. I can feel the coolness of him. I glide along the edge of him, sliding along his shaft without allowing him to penetrate me. Not yet.

"My Faith," Loki says in a low moan. "You are torturing me."

"If it makes you feel better, I'm torturing myself, too." And such sweet torture it is.

Suddenly, a new sensation pushes against my sensitive skin. I gasp, looking down. While Loki's blue penis had been smooth before, now rippling ridges cascaded down his shaft.

Shapeshifting, I think, remembering the legends. Loki has the power to make illusions real, to change his form. And he is very specifically changing for my pleasure.

I bounce my fingers over his hard, ridged cock, sucking in my breath, my heart racing with desire.

He wants to claim me. I want to claim him.

But first, I'm claiming myself.

I reach up, stroking the side of his face. My

fingers glide from his sharp cheekbones to rake his soft, white hair. I pause at the horns jutting from his head, gently feeling them, my hand following the way they curve. Carefully, I grip one of his horns. I glance down at him. Loki's eyes are liquid, intense in a way I have never seen them before. This doesn't hurt him. It's turning him on even more.

Holding onto one of his horns with one hand, I move my other over my body, inches from his face and rapt attention. He emboldens me, and the movements I make, using his horn as leverage, are lithe, dance-like. I briefly took a pole-dancing class in college, just a lark that some of the other girls took far more seriously than I did. I never understood the way I could make my body move around something so stiff and unyielding, but now I do. Loki holds himself perfectly still, easily balancing his weight against mine as my hips swing and my breasts sway before him.

I stroke my left hand up, over his horn, and my right hand down, into my slick folds, rubbing into my clit.

My breath comes out in quick pants. This teasing, delayed gratification is driving us both mad, but he watches me press into my clit, a button of pleasure that makes my whole body jerk in response. I let myself fall into his lap, not bothering with any effort to remain standing. My knuckles brush against his cock, but I don't let up, winding that coil of pressure in my body tight enough that I almost get myself off.

"Do you want . . ." I pant, catching my breath as I look up into Loki's eyes, hard with desire. "Do you want me to come all over you?"

He swallows. He looks as if he wants to eat me whole.

"Or," I say, my hand working furiously over my clit, "would you rather come inside me?"

The way I have his hands bound means that he cannot grab me and control my body. I am in control.

"Take me," Loki growls. "Claim me."

I need no other invitation. I arch up and drive his cock into me, my pussy clenching around his hard shaft. He bucks up off the floor, pounding into me as I wrap my legs around his waist as much as I'm able.

His huge cock stretches me past what I would have thought possible, and the ridges he'd added hit in *all* the right spots. My body pulses around him, and I wiggle, arching my back and forcing my hips down so I can take his full, considerable length into me. He twitches, his cock hitting a spot that connects to my clit, and my breath comes out in a soft mewling gasp.

And that is when he *roars*, loud enough to rattle the glass in the windows, cold cum shooting into me in a way that sends delicious ice along every nerve in my body. I collapse against Loki's chest, my pussy clenching around him as wave after wave of pleasure rocks through me. Unable to contain himself, Loki jerks his arms, the leather snapping at his wrists. I would be impressed by this feat, but I'm too busy feeling the way he grips my hips, the way he bends his body to claim me in a kiss, his tongue darting past my lips eagerly even as I feel his cum spurting into me.

CHAPTER 12
LOKI

had intended to bathe and dress Faith myself, and this room is filled with everything I would need to do so — but the moment we both come, Faith trembling in my lap and my cock throbbing inside her warm cunt, Faith stands off of me. She hisses as the ridges slide out of her sensitive walls, and pride swells in my chest.

I start to rise.

She clucks her tongue. "Ah-ah. Did I say you could get up?"

The game is not yet over.

I grin at her, eyes darkening, a warm flush spreading across my chest. I dare not speak, not even now, all of my focus on staying pliant for her.

I am not used to being the one commanded.

But gazing up at her, seeing the sheer confidence

that radiates off her body, I feel an old side of me opening, one long gone dormant. One from lifetimes ago, when I could afford mischief and joy, when I had space to think of things other than survival and ruling.

Faith finds a washbasin next to the fireplace, a pot of water already heating where I had intended to bathe her. She readies it herself, and as she dips a cloth into the steaming water, she watches me.

My eyes have never left her. My grin remains, feral and devilish, and she shakes her head with a smile.

"Never have you looked more like your carvings than you do now," she says half to herself.

She trails the wet cloth over her breasts. A droplet of water runs over her nipple.

I am on the floor still, obedient, but my wrists are no longer bound, and she gave no commands about what powers I can use.

A flick of my hand, and an illusion of me appears in front of her, naked, cock hard and at attention.

Faith jumps, then laughs. "Resorting to your tricks, are you? There will be punishments for that."

Punishments, I can handle. I crave, actually.

The illusion of me steps closer to her.

Another appears behind her.

A third just next to her.

Faith's eyes jump to each of them, all three with my sizable hard cock pointing towards her.

She continues to wash herself, dipping into the hot water, letting the towel trail down her soft skin. There is a slight flash of calculation in her eyes as she looks from me to the illusion behind her. He reaches for her, and I know she can feel him. I can feel her through him, the way he trails his fingers down her arm, leaving goosebumps in his wake. The head of his cock prods her ass, and she gasps.

"How many of me can you handle, my Faith?" is all I manage to growl.

I am regressing to my most base of natures.

And I cannot get enough.

Faith gasps again as the illusion in front closes in on her too. The cloth slips from her fingers.

"I am trying to get ready for *your* feast," she tells me, but her words end on a breathy exhale as the illusion behind grabs her thighs and lifts her, spreading her wide for the other two. "*Loki* — !"

I grin wider. My cock throbs and the illusions match it, the tips identical with precum, still coated in her drying juices.

My fingers tense into the stones of the floor, the only thing keeping me from diving across the room and adding a fourth *me* to the mix.

"I have decided," all three illusions say in my

voice, "that you are an aphrodisiac, my Faith. Your very aura consumes me. Your body was made for my cock."

She is so focused on the illusions in front of her, the way one is staring hungrily at her spread cunt and the other reaches for her nipple, that she has forgotten the one holding her.

It is he that I make slam into her open, dripping pussy, his long cock filling her already soaked and stretched hole. She screams, bright and surprised, but the angle of his cock has her throwing her head back against his chest. Another minor shift of my hands, and I create the same ridges on his cock that drove her to utmost pleasure, pushing and rubbing every corner of her walls.

"Loki — this is — *cheating* — " she says between his powerful thrusts.

"I'm not touching you," I say from the floor. "I haven't moved at all."

"*Loki* — "

"Too much, my Faith?" the three illusions ask. "Say the word, pet. Or don't."

One of the other two steps closer.

Faith feels his hands on her stomach and throws me — the real me — a startled look.

I wait. The one holding her continues to thrust, readying her, but I hesitate, giving her time to process what I want, what she has brought out in me.

Her face is flushed, sweaty even in the chilly air, her skin beautifully pink and ripened from my ravenous needs.

But she nods.

She *nods*.

And where I was feral before, I am a beast now.

The illusion spreads her folds, showing me the way one ridged cock already slams in and out, blue skin glistening with her moisture.

"Fill her," I snarl, bent forward on the floor, breaths coming in tight, painful gasps.

The illusion obeys. He first slips a finger in her alongside the other cock, and Faith writhes, breath-less and beautiful.

"Too — too much — " she whines, but she does not say the safe word, and so the illusion presses on, opening her hole, the other cock slowing its thrusts as she is stretched, fingers working her, pulling, softening.

The noises she makes already. The whimpers and moans and pleas.

I am heady with her sounds.

The illusion angles his cock alongside the ridged one, and slowly, *slowly*, begins to push his head alongside the length of the other.

Faith goes utterly limp. I can feel her lithe and lean and fully surrendering to me, though she is the one who could stop this with a word, with a look. That surrender gives the illusion the space it needs — his cock glides inside of her, and she makes a keening, brittle sound, like need, like desire, like desperation undone.

"*Loki* . . ." she moans, and it is music.

The illusions begin moving in tandem. One thrusts in, one pulls out, two cocks filling her tight, sweet cunt.

Another twitch of my fingers.

I am all mischief now, pushing her to the brink as I create ridges on the other cock as well.

Faith's whines turn to high-pitched wails, sensation incarnate.

The third illusion is all roaming hands, feeling where I know she loves. Hands tweak her pebbled nipples, pinching and rolling the tight buds until she is crying with pleasure, sensation overcome. She begins to tremble, and before I can even have my illusion touch her clit, she comes, fast and hard, as the illusions continue thrusting.

"We will not tire, my Faith," the illusions say. "We are yours to use. Yours to fuck for as long as you demand."

Her head is thrown back, her body arched so her

breasts are on full display. And because she has given no command, the third illusion continues to play, teasing and tugging her nipples, and finally bending down to take one in his mouth.

I feel the swell of her breast, taste the sweetness of her sweaty skin; and I feel the thrust of each cock inside of her, so impossibly tight that I cannot fathom how she is taking this, but take it she does; and then she begins rocking her hips, riding these cocks, *my* cocks, and where I am seated on the floor, I come. Great streams of seed arch over the floor, my hips rocking along with hers. I have the third illusion pinch her clit through the folds and rub it as he suckles her breast, and she *screams* with orgasm, a cry that burrows deep into my soul.

She is just coming down from it when I cross the room, flinging myself on her body as the illusions fade. I catch her, cradle her to me, bending to my knees to kiss across her shoulders, between her breasts, licking away sweat from her perfect, raptured form.

I think I tell her all the things I am feeling, all I have been feeling since she arrived.

I think I worship her, praising her body, her mind, her invigorating soul.

I think, but I am unaware, delirious in her, because of her.

She dissolves into me, kissing me in return, and the two of us fall to the floor, a tangle of limbs and promises and new beginnings.

This woman has remade me in the span of a day.

It will destroy me to let her leave.

———

We miss the evening feast.

Unsurprisingly.

Faith falls fast asleep in the preparation room, the kind of deep, resonant sleep that only comes after hard labor, and I manage to dress her simply and carry her back to my chambers just as the feast is winding down.

"Tomorrow," I promise her sleeping form, because we will have tomorrow, if not another day; how long will it take for my councilors to inspect the portal and return? Days, at least.

At least.

I tuck her beneath the blankets on my bed and swear that I will spend a full hour tomorrow *not* fucking her, so she truly *can* see the feast. We will kill each other if we keep up this level of love-making.

But oh, what a glorious way to die.

CHAPTER 13
FAITH

have no idea how much I sleep, but it is wondrous.

By the time my eyes finally open, I discover that I no longer have that strange sensation of waking up somewhere I don't recognize. As I stretch, I feel the furs on Loki's bed and know they are his. I brush up against his body, and I'm aware it is him.

It feels like home.

"Awake, my Faith?" Loki asks in a low, sensuous rumble. His deep voice vibrates through the bed, making me instantly wet. I roll over, looking into his big eyes.

"Awake," I confirm. "And really well rested." I'm not sure which I appreciate more, the sex or the sleep after. My stomach rumbles. "But I'm also hungry."

"That can easily be remedied," Loki says. "We

missed last night's feast, but are just in time for the one tonight."

My stomach does another lurch, this time nothing to do with hunger. Emotions war inside me. On the one hand, I'm starving. On the other, I recall some of the frost giants' initial hesitation toward me. Seeing them at the crafting stations and throughout the village was one thing, but at a feast?

But also a *feast*. The number of times I've longed to see a *real* Viking feast! But then again, I would not be able to do much observing if they were all too wary of me. But also —

"My Faith?" Loki asks. "What troubles you?"

My stomach rumbles again. "I'm *starving*."

Loki laughs. "Then let us feast."

He gets out of bed, giving me a fine display of his ass. I recall that yesterday, we'd been about to get me dressed for the feast when we . . . well . . .

Heat flushes my body.

Loki looks behind him. He raises an eyebrow at me. "I could avoid another feast."

"No!" I say, laughing. "I actually really want to go!"

"In that case . . ." he says, his voice trailing off only a little reluctantly. He takes a tunic off a peg and starts to get dressed himself.

I jump out of bed and notice that the clothing that

had been in the dressmakers' room is now neatly folded on the bench at the foot of Loki's bed. I approach a moss green dress first, lacing down each side. It's beautiful in its simplicity, but when I come closer, I see some of the finest embroidery I've ever witnessed etched along the hem and around the neck, shooting down both long sleeves of the arms. The thread is almost the same shade as the cloth, but the pattern of the embroidery is intricate, two snakes twining around each other, forming roughly an "S" shape as they bite their tails, repeated all along the dress. This is a common symbol of Loki, with lots of archeological evidence.

Interspersed throughout the snakes is another repeating pattern: the rune Kenaz. It looks a little like the "less than" symbol in mathematics, a "V" shape on its side, pointing left. This is the rune roughly associated with torches, but it's more than that. Flickering torchlight provides both light and long shadows of darkness; it can aid you or it can give your position away to the enemy; it helps but only for a certain amount of time before it goes out and burns your hands.

It's the perfect rune for Loki.

This dress is not some cast-off refitted for me. It's been made for me, a symbol of how Loki has claimed *me.* It's a sign to everyone in the feast, everyone in Jotunheim — I am *his.*

I know the proper order of Viking garments, designed for both warmth and functionality, so I put on the undergarment first, a warm woolen smock. There's more material in the smock than what I typically wear to bed, but there are no panties. I knew this; panties are a relatively modern concept, but there's something sensual about the idea of being so heavily clothed and yet completely accessible in the most private area.

My eyes flick to Loki. He watches me as I get dressed, his eyes molten. No doubt the same thought has crossed his wicked mind.

The moss green dress slips over my head. It's designed to be cinched in at the waist with the lacing across either side, so I twist my body, tugging at the strings to draw the dress tighter.

"Let me." Loki's voice is deep and he pads barefoot over the stone floor to me.

He has helped me get undressed rather a lot over the past few days. He's quite good at ripping my clothes off. But as his fingers pull the laces, carefully drawing the material close to my body so that it's snug but not tight, he acts with a gentleness I have never seen from him before.

I touch one of the Kenaz runes on my sleeve. He is the torch that lit up my dark and lonely world, and when his light is gone from my life, I fear that I will be burned to ash.

"There." Loki steps back, looking at his handiwork on my dress. It fits perfectly, and even though the cloth is drawn tight around my midriff, I do a small twirl, the skirt flaring at my ankles.

Beside the dress, an apron has been folded for me to don. The only person I know who wears an apron in real life is Maya at the coffee shop. She has a rainbow array of linen aprons, a different color for each day of the week, all of them dusted in flour and sugar as she concocts different cakes and pastries for our Study Group sessions.

This apron is different. For Vikings, clothing was entirely handmade, from shearing to spinning to weaving to sewing. Dresses required a lot of material, so aprons were worn over top of the dress as an accent and fashion statement, as well as protection over the more labor-intensive dress. While my dress is moss green, the apron that goes with it is vivid emerald, with golden threads creating intertwined snakes on the bib. The bright green material flows all the way to the hem of my dress with a panel of gold along the bottom.

The straps on the apron, however, are loose. I look

around for pins to secure them — richer Viking women used elaborate brooches as another status symbol.

"Here." Loki holds out a tray to me, with half a dozen pairs of brooches on display. Silver and gold, bronze and iron, each of these brooches looks brand new, gleaming up at me.

I touch a pair of round iron brooches adorned with the Degaz rune. Degaz symbolized dawn and new beginnings, and that seems . . . hopeful in light of my situation. But dawn also reminds me of sunset. So I leave them in the box.

My hands shift to two golden brooches that twist and curl. I glance from their shape up to Loki and gasp. A knowing smirk spreads over his face.

These brooches were designed to look like Loki's horns. Golden instead of ivory, true, but they are the exact shape, only miniaturized. I pluck them from the tray and use the horns to affix the apron straps over my dress. They rest at the top of my breasts, heavy, a constant reminder that he claimed me, and I claimed him.

———

Nerves twist inside me like twin snakes as I follow Loki from his chambers to the feast hall. Feasts were an important element of Viking culture, I know that. I go over all the academic facts I have memorized about Viking mead halls, the way they worked as seats of power, community buildings, fortresses against assault . . .

And then I step inside.

Nothing — *nothing* — could have ever prepared me for the feast hall spread before me.

When I walked into Jotunheim before, I was struck by how community-like the entire area was. It went beyond my studies — there were cohesive working groups, clear friendships and camaraderie, a sense of love among all the people. Jotunheim was their *home,* and they loved it and everyone in it. They worked and lived together.

And at the mead hall, they drink and cheer and take that idea of a loving community to a *whole* other level.

Nobody could embody the idea of "work hard, play hard" quite like a Viking. Tankards are raised, foamy heads of mead sloshing over the sides. Platters of food that are likely far too heavy for me to even pick up are slung on the tables: glistening and juicy roast pig, mutton doused in thick gravy, some sort of bird that has its feathers fanned around the edge of the plate, a charred salmon that looks as long as I am tall. There is dancing on one side of the hall, vigorously swirling dresses and men catching the women before spinning them out again. Some people are singing — not drunken slurs, but truly beautiful music accompanied by string instruments. Sweet, honeyed scents of cakes weave through the hall, a promise of more deliciousness to come.

Loki starts toward the head table, raised above the main floor. He waits when I don't move.

"My Faith," he says in a low voice I can barely hear. "You do not walk behind me. You walk beside me."

I rush forward, my petite legs working twice as hard under my green skirt to keep up with Loki's long stride.

As I walk at his arm to the main table, a hush spreads out, the silence stark in the wake of such boisterous feasting before.

Loki seems perfectly at ease as he approaches the head table, a relaxed smile on his face. He likes the attention, I realize.

He looks out at the crowd, his eyebrow cocking mischievously. No — it's not the attention he loves. It's the disruption.

Loki likes chaos.

Jotunheim may have become a perfect, idyllic utopia for the frost giants, a place of placid peace. But as much as he values the safety of his people, he has longed for the chance to shake things up. For a taste of his old ways, his old danger. To create turmoil and confusion and —

Excitement.

That is what lights up his face as he looks from the crowd of his people to me.

I am exciting. New and different and unexpected.

A thrill chases up my spine. I am not used to being valued for what I am. At my university — from most of my teachers to my ex-boyfriend — I was valued for what I could do. It's such a fine distinction that I never really noticed it before.

Or perhaps I have never been loved like this before, loved for who I am, treasured because I was different, all the more valuable for not fitting into a mold. Maybe it won't last, or maybe I'll have to leave Jotunheim before my newness wears off, but for now, I cherish it.

Breathlessly, I take the seat Loki offers me, at his right-hand side, the place of highest honor.

A female voice from the crowd shouts, "Dróttning!" The silence broken, the feast resumes, cheering mingled with music, laughter and joy creating their own rhythm.

I smile down at my clasped hands in my lap. *Dróttning* is an Old Norse word. It could mean "mistress," which it must be obvious to everyone in the feast hall applies to my relationship with Loki. But unlike modern society, it's not a word filled with derision.

Because the alternative meaning of "dróttning" — the more common meaning, actually — is "queen."

CHAPTER 14
LOKI

My Faith is a queen.

I had longed to see her properly made up in all the grandeur she deserves, but the finished product is beyond what even I had imagined. She sits now with a group of women who braid greenery into her hair, creating a similar style most frost giants wear, though where we put ornamentation along our horns, they simply weave more beads and berries into her locks.

As they finish, she stands and turns to me, and I am struck dumb with her beauty.

The green of her gown gives her skin a polished glow, or perhaps that is the firelight of the feast hall, or the way she blushes under my predatory appraisal. Her thick hair is woven back from her face and each sprig of plant and dangle of gold enhances the regality in her bearing.

My people had called her dróttning without my prodding.

She is that — a queen.

My queen.

Faith crosses the space between where the women had styled her hair and my table, where I lean against the wood, a mug of mead in hand. She smiles up at me, and I think she may speak — but a song begins across the room, one fast and powerful, all heavy percussions and thrusting beats.

Her face lightens, and she gapes up at me. "Loki! This song — I've seen the sheet music, but I've never *heard* it — what instruments are they using?" She pushes onto her toes, craning her neck to see, and it is impossible not to tumble headfirst into her enthusiasm.

I take her arm. "Dance with me, my Faith."

Her fascination pulls back, and she gives me a soft, enrapturing smile. "The king of Jotunheim has asked me to dance? How did I get so lucky?"

"It is not luck." I bend down to her, lips tracing the shell of her ear. "It is fate. I have always been yours."

I am getting too bold with my words to her. But I am finding it harder to care.

"Come," I tell her. I lift her into my arms, chest swelling with her squeal of giddiness, and I rush the two of us to the dance floor, where other couples make room.

The song carries us through traditional moves that Faith picks up easily. She explains at each one how she studied similar dances, and how she cannot believe the musicians have an actual skalmejen instrument, and if there are any dances specific to Jotunheim?

Yes, I tell her. I will show you those dances someday.

I will get you a skalmejen and teach you how to play.

I make promise after promise, and Faith accepts each one, her joy radiating and intoxicating.

We leave the dance floor once we are both breathless and sweat-sheened, and I feed her meats and pastries and she exclaims over the cooking. The rest of the evening I spend on her heels, watching her speak with the musicians, and the chefs, and the seamstresses, peppering them with questions and fawning over their skill.

I can see my people falling in love with her.

Does she know we are slipping under her spell? I do not suspect so. She is merely being herself, genuine and curious and humble, and by the end of the night, I know all of Jotunheim is in the beginnings of being at her mercy.

Faith sways with exhaustion as I lead her back to my room. I lift her, cradling her against my chest, and she lays her head on my shoulder.

"That was magical, Loki," she whispers, her breath warm on my neck.

"You will have that magic again tomorrow," I tell her.

"And it's always like this? Wonders every day." She yawns. "Because of you. You gave them this."

"They have built it for themselves."

"No." She shifts up, coming out of her sleepy fog to fix her gaze on me as I push into my room.

Our room.

"No?" I kick the door shut.

"*You* gave them this," Faith repeats. "You have created utopia, Loki. Do you know how many gods strive for that, only to fall disastrously short? And you've done it."

I set Faith on the edge of the bed and begin pulling the ornamentation out of her hair. Sprigs of holly scent the air between us with earthy green.

"Utopia," I whisper. "Days ago, I would have disagreed with you."

"Hmm?" Faith moans the question, leaning into the way I gently rub her scalp, pulling free her hair.

"It did not feel like a utopia until you arrived."

Silence hangs. My fingers go still against her, but I pause for only a moment before I begin undoing the ties on her dress, her apron, unpinning her brooches.

I feel her eyes on the side of my face, lit by the fire already burning in the hearth.

"How can you really mean that?" Faith whispers.

I maneuver the gown up, freeing her until she is in only the thin underdress.

Then I kneel before her, and I meet her gaze, bare and open and true.

"I created this home for my people," I say. "And I found meaning in their joy — for a time. I was ashamed to admit that I was beginning to feel empty here. How could one feel unsettled when I had achieved what I had worked so long for? I was searching, searching for I knew not what. And then — you." I touch her cheek. "I truly believe the portal chose to bring you to me, my Faith. I truly believe it was fate. And I know you are destined to return to your Earth, and I will do everything in my power to see you happy and safe — but know that you have changed me utterly, and I will rip a new portal in space and time if it means seeing you again."

Faith's eyes tear. She closes them, leaning into my

touch, and her lips twist in a smile of disbelief. "You'll come to see me on Earth?"

"Or," I push, "if you wished to stay here, at my side, you would be welcome."

Her eyes slip open. She stares at me for a long moment, so long that I feel my heart pause in the silence, entirely frozen under this woman's power.

She sniffs and shakes her head, breaking the spell. "Stay or go — I'm *mortal*, Loki. How would this even work?"

"You have seen my power — you think I do not possess the ability to lengthen a mortal's life?"

"This is just — " She stops, the heels of her palms digging into her eyes. "Do we have to talk about this now? I just want the magic to last. I'm not ready for . . . reality."

My heart squeezes. I brush her hair over her shoulder. "The magic will remain. No decisions must be made now. I am sorry," my voice catches, "for bringing it up. This evening was yours, and I — "

Faith puts her hand on my lips, silencing me, and the act still drives a feral spike through me. "Don't apologize. Tonight — these past days — they've all been *perfect*. It's like a dream."

I push closer to her, letting my lips rest over hers. "Then don't wake up, my Faith."

I kiss her, a gentle palpation of our mouths, before

I work my lips down her neck, across her collarbone, following the rise of her breast through her under-dress. Her nipple is soft beneath the fabric, but she gasps, her fingers coming to knot around my horns as I push lower.

Wordlessly, I lift the hem of her underdress and spread her legs for me. The firelight flickers orange and yellow on her perfect cunt, and I begin lapping at it in slow, steady pulses.

"Loki," Faith moans, gripping my horns still. "Loki — "

I delve into her folds, arching my tongue deep, deep into her warm hole, and she mewls, though I can feel the tension in her voice, in the way she holds onto me.

These days have been ripe with magic, but reality is looming, and I feel as though I have broken it for us both. When she leaves — and she will leave — I must give her all the reasons to have me still, to believe that this dream can continue after she wakes up. I will shape change into whatever she desires, I will mask illusions over any situation to make it palatable for Earth — whatever she needs. Whatever she wants.

I just hope that at the end of this, what she wants is me.

———

I fill the next days with as much Jotunheim magic as possible. Which is not hard — Faith is mesmerized by my city, and my people are likewise mesmerized by her; and through her, I am falling back in love with Jotunheim, with our ways and customs and life, and so I do not even have to *try* to create magic. Faith emits it wherever she goes.

We visit the village every day, and Faith chooses to spend much of her time in the weaving courtyard, where she is learning how to use a loom.

We feast every evening, and dance, and Faith begins learning how to play some of the instruments.

I carry her back to our bed every night, and we make love before the fire, our bodies knotted on the furs, and as she writhes beneath me, I kiss promises into her skin.

It is, as she said, a utopia.

But a shadow ever hangs over this utopia, though this time it is not my own growing restlessness.

My group of councilors has not yet returned from the portal. If there was a problem, they may have needed to stay to properly study it; but even so, by the fifth day since Faith's arrival, my unease is a beast of iron and unquiet, and I watch Faith get dressed for the evening feast with a tight jaw and knotted fists.

Fingers touch my forehead, and I realize my brow had been furrowed as well.

Faith stands before me where I sit on the bed, her head tipped in concern. "What's wrong?"

I take her hips in my hands, bracketing her between my legs. "Are you happy, my Faith?"

"Very."

"Then what could be wrong?"

But she levels a look at me. How quickly she has learned to see through my facade, one I had worn quite successfully around my people for years.

"Loki," she puts emphasis into my name, and I can't help but cut a smirk at her.

"Am I in trouble?" I cock an eyebrow and drag her closer, letting her feel the hard length of me against her thighs. "I do believe I need a punishment. It has been four long hours since I tasted you — the feast can wait, if you insist, dróttning."

I lean in, angling to bite her neck, but Faith locks a hand around one of my horns and pulls my face back.

A growl rumbles in my throat. She has learned how easily I can be manipulated by holding my horns, and I am hard pressed not to dissolve into my feral nature when she manhandles me.

"Loki," she says again. Her face goes from teasing to severe. "It's the portal, isn't it? They should have been back by now."

I lean away, my hands still on her hips, keeping her close to me. "I hadn't minded that they took extra time," I whisper.

Faith releases my horn, her hand coming to cover my fingers on her body. "Me too."

My eyes flash to her. These days I have spent pouring promises on her, and she has yet to make such promises in return.

"It does not have to end," I remind her softly.

She stiffens. "Loki. The portal. What are we going to do about it?"

I bite the inside of my cheek. Her stubbornness will bend. It has to. We will soon need to have a real discussion about a future beyond these days, though I understand her hesitation. My own chest is a knot of fear.

I stand, keeping a hold of her, unable to let her go for even a moment. "I will investigate what has taken them so long." I kiss her temple quickly. "Join the feast. I will be back tomorrow."

I will need supplies. Weapons.

Faith grabs onto my forearms as I turn. "Wait — I'm coming with you."

I whip a glare down at her. "Absolutely not. You will stay here."

"This whole thing is because of *me*. Because of *my* presence here. I'm going with you."

There's a weight in her words. Does she feel guilty? For the tear weakening, for the disruption?

"Is that why you hesitate with me," I start, "because you feel responsible for being here?"

Faith's jaw sets. "I don't understand why I'm here or how it happened at all. And if I broke a centuries-old barrier because of a *research trip* — " She straightens, already starting to pull off her feast gown. "I'm going. And we're going to figure out what's going on. *Together*."

"Faith." I follow her across the room. Normally, I would rejoice to watch her undress, but I grab her arm to stop her. "You are so small. Fragile. I cannot—"

"I am *not* fragile, Loki."

"Not — that was incorrect. I mean — you are not a frost giant. The tundra is no place for a human."

"I have my old supplies. I can make the trek. That's not an issue. You can't keep me here, and I—"

"I won't lose you."

Faith stops, half out of her gown.

She looks up at me, and for the first time, there is

vulnerability in her eyes. I go perfectly still, afraid if I move at all, she will break out of it.

"I won't lose you, either," she says, and I am afloat. "I love you, Loki. And I won't let you face this alone. It probably isn't anything to worry about, anyway, right? Your council just ran into an issue they couldn't solve. We'll find them out there, and we'll — "

"You love me," I repeat.

Faith's cheeks darken. Her eyes tear, and as she looks away, I catch her face in my hand and kiss her, the force sending her back until she is pinned to the wall, my body holding her aloft.

I kiss her with all the force of how she has changed me, pushing at the barrier she has erected between us, willing it to fall. She winds her arms around my neck, and I feel her resistance crumble.

"I love you," she says into me, and I am undone utterly. I would fall to my knees at her feet if she was not held up in my arms; I would cry joy to the sky if her lips were not sweeter than mead.

"I love you," I say, though she knows; she must know, with how I have worshipped her.

"Together, then?" Faith knots her fist in my hair, holding her forehead to mine.

My stomach cramps with a familiar need — wanting to keep her to myself, to keep her hidden and away and *safe*. But letting her out into Jotunheim endeared her to my people.

Perhaps letting her come now will be the best result yet again.

I nuzzle into her hair, the deep, rich smell of her at the base of her neck. "Together, my Faith."

CHAPTER 15
FAITH

I don't like my old clothes.

I understand why they are important. The frost giants' bodies are adapted to the cold, and while the palace and city of Jotunheim are like a typical winter day — cold without a cloak or fires in the hearth — the further we get from the city center, the more arctic the mountains become. Even Loki wraps his woolen cloak tighter, wind whipping at the hem. My arctic thermal gear is more than appreciated, but the cold bites at me, stinging my skin. If I were still wearing the clothes from Jotunheim, I would be getting frostbite in my fingers.

So, I am grateful for my gear.

But I also hate it.

Because it reminds me of all that I am not: not a frost giant, not good enough to truly live here.

And it reminds me of all that I am: human. Mortal. Temporary.

Loki said there was magic to lengthen my lifespan . . . I dispel the thought from my head. We both said a lot of things, but my sandcastle dreams are crumbling now.

As I follow behind Loki on the narrow trail leading to the rift, I try to focus on the situation at hand. It is important that Loki discover what made the portal fail. Not many people come to Jan Mayan Island, true, but it's used by scientists and sometimes the military. If the portal is broken, it's too risky to expose it to the people of my world.

I look up at Loki's back, his dark green cloak billowing as the winds pick up.

His world and my world have to remain separated.

It's for the best, I remind myself. It would be the discovery of a lifetime to expose Jotunheim to the world, but I would never, ever do that to these wonderful people. To Loki. They're safe here.

Without me.

We hike for hours, the passage so arduous that Loki has to lift me bodily over some boulders, carry me across narrow passes. The climb has my thighs aching, my lungs burning in the thin, cold air. I can see now why no one expected the expedition to return in a day or three. We are essentially scaling a mountain, and I'm only grateful that I was passed out when Loki first brought me from this place.

As we near the summit, Loki stops. I turn at the crest of a craggy, icy ridge. I look behind me, the settlement lost among the snow and trees in the distance. The sky here looks more like water this high up, clouds that could be mistaken for ice, a wavering sheen to the blue that looks like ripples on the lake, and I'm reminded how I fell through the water to get to this point.

When Loki still doesn't move, I maneuver around him to see what has caused him to grow so still and quiet.

"Loki?" I ask in a soft voice.

And I see the dead.

Bright red blood splatters over the icy rocks, vivid and grotesque. The bodies all seem to have fallen from a great height, the arms and legs jutting at odd angles, heads twisting unnaturally, torsos splattered over the cold, some half-strewn on the frozen surface of the nearby pond.

A scream that is made of horror at the site bubbles up my throat.

And then I see a face I recognize and an entirely different sort of scream rips from me.

The body closest to me, with eyes wide open, glassy and staring — is Dr. Phillips.

Loki tries to hold me back, but he cannot. Gulping for air as panic rises in my chest, I fall painfully to my knees at Dr. Phillips's side.

She was the leader of the Study Group, the person who cared about women not being lost in academia so much that she sacrificed part of her career to stay as a professor and ensure the group's survival. But beyond that, she was my mentor, practically a mother to me, someone who always believed in me, always pushed me to be better, always caught me when I fell. I gasp for breath, my eyes blurring.

What happened? I want to ask, but I cannot get the words out, no more than she could answer.

I cast my eyes around to the other bodies, desperately hoping what I fear isn't true.

But it is.

There's Josie, her back broken over a sharp rock. Renee, who seems to have been hurled from the sky headfirst. Marie, arms and legs akimbo, her open eyes reflecting the clouds. More, more. Some are turned away from me, but I recognize Ursula's long braids. Cate's red hair. Elanor's glasses, snapped in half and covered in blood.

The Study Group wasn't just a study group. It

was a sisterhood in the deepest sense of the word; the girls in the group loved me, and I loved them.

And if I went missing, they would have come to find me. I know that on a bone-deep level — they would have come for me.

But . . .

I look up and scream at the sky. I can almost picture it. Dr. Phillips organizing and funding the flights for an expedition to check on me when I went missing. How many days has it been? Perhaps time works differently in Jotunheim. She would have come for me, though — they all would have. Dr. Phillips knew how dangerous my expedition was. She worried. And the others would not have simply let our professor go to the Arctic.

There must have been some clue — tracks, perhaps, or an item I'd dropped — as I fell through the portal. And they followed me.

But while the portal had gently landed me in Jotunheim, cold, yes, but otherwise unharmed . . .

My friends, the closest people I have to family, fell and broke like shattered dolls on the craggy cliffs.

My chest caves in, and my body breaks in sobs. What the fuck have I been doing? Fucking around, literally, with a god, but to what end? I went missing, and the people I love tried to find me, and now they are all *dead*, miserably, painfully, horrifically *dead*.

I feel a gentle hand on my back, and I'm too broken to jerk away, even though I don't deserve any comfort. Distantly, through my own sobbing, I'm aware of Loki saying my name. Then his hands close over my shoulders, and he tries to pull me from Dr. Phillips's body.

"No!" I sob. I deserve this grief. I caused this pain. I deserve to die here with them. And even though a part of me can hear Dr. Phillips's soft voice telling me that's not true, that's only my sorrow talking, I cannot help but sink into my grief the same way I sank into the portal, only this time, I think, it may kill me.

And then some of Loki's words penetrate through the cloud of pain. He's no longer trying to say my name. He's telling me . . .

"This isn't real."

He's right. It can't be real. But it is. They're right here in front of me. The blood, the bodies —

And then it registers. Loki was able to craft illusions, powerful ones. Ones that made it seem as if he ripped the throat out of the dissenter on his council. What was his name? Fenrir. That had looked real, too, even to Fenrir, but it hadn't been.

I turn, looking up at the blue frost giant I've fallen in love with, feeling hope.

Loki's face is framed by sorrow, too. "This is an

illusion," he tells me softly, holding his hand out to help me stand. I follow him, taking several paces back with him. We look out at the craggy, icy rocks, and Loki waves his hands.

Some of the bodies disappear, but three remain, growing longer, wider, bluer. A horn and a broken one sprout from the closest body — the one that had looked like Dr. Phillips. Loki breathes out a sad sigh and says the name of one of the frost giants who'd been on the expedition to find and fix the portal between our realms.

"Sigyn," he says, a prayer on his lips.

He's dead.

The illusion made the bodies look like my friends, but it did not change the fact that they were dead bodies.

There is both aching relief in my heart and a new kind of sorrow. I did not know this group well, but Loki did. His cold eyes shift from body to body, naming each one, his voice low, choked with grief. The pain I feel now is not my own heart breaking, but the pain of watching someone I love have his heart broken. It's a different sort of pain, but still sharp.

Now that my heart has settled and my panic has stilled, I also notice something else — the portal. A planar rift cuts through a massive boulder like a geode, but instead of crystals lining it, cool light glows and swirls, like the aurora borealis. I do not recall falling through this portal, but that must have been what happened before Loki found me.

But why are the frost giants dead in front of it?

"What happened?" I whisper, but Loki shakes his head.

"A better question — who is missing?"

I look at the bodies again. There is one I would have recognized — Fenrir, the dissenter. He is not there.

A slow clap echoes over the silent mountain top. A slow fucking clap. The pretentious asshole.

Fenrir moves out from behind a boulder. "You know," he says, a chuckle in his voice. "That was quite an entertaining show you put on, little human."

He means my grief. My breaking heart. It *amused* him.

"What did you do?" Loki growls. Power radiates off him, but he keeps it in check, suppressing his rage so he can discover the truth.

"The others said the portal was just fine. Not broken. It just 'let' the little girl through." Fenrir snarls the word, "let," as if it disgusts him.

"Why did you not then return to the palace?" Loki says, his voice a careful monotone.

"Oh, that's what the others wanted to do." Fenrir

looks down at the bodies of his companions with a little smile on his face, like they were children playing and not corpses rotting on the ice. He turns his face toward Loki, his expression shifting rapidly fiercer. "The portal let *her* through, but it won't let *me* out."

"That's because she belongs here," Loki said, and at this, finally, his voice breaks with emotion.

"The portal did not just gift you a fuck toy!" Fenrir roars.

This makes Loki's whole body clench, his muscles hard, rigid lines as he restrains himself from ripping Fenrir's throat out for real. But I'm still processing what they've said.

The portal let me through.

I *belong* here.

Not just as Loki's toy, no matter what Fenrir says. More than that.

I belong *here*.

"Why did you make the bodies look like my friends?" I ask hollowly. No matter what beef Fenrir has with Loki, it seems like a particularly cruel twist of the knife to me.

Fenrir snorts in disgust. It's Loki who answers: "He is not as skilled at illusions as I am."

"Could have fooled me," I say quietly, still picturing Dr. Phillips's glassy eyes.

Loki shakes his head. "He pulled images of people you loved from your mind and shadow-projected them onto the bodies."

"They were supposed to remind you of *your* filthy world," Fenrir growls. "So that you went back to the portal and opened it."

"And then you would go through with her," Loki says. It was an imperfect solution, but if Loki hadn't been with me, it almost would have worked. There are lots of my friends here, but not the whole Study Group. I couldn't risk Maya leading another expedition of more of my friends out here. Or really, any human life — if my friends had truly been smashed on these rocks, I would have gone through to ensure no one else ever attempted to go through the portal.

But Loki showed me the truth.

"There's something about *her* that the portal let through," Fenrir says, his blazing eyes raking over my body in a way that feels like a violation.

Because it *is* a violation.

I think back to the time I met him, the way he leered at me, his eyes penetrating. Loki had told me about magic, how he was a master of illusions, but that most of the other frost giants could create similar manifestations. He had told me that some possessed other abilities, such as influencing emotions or picking memories from someone's mind. Fenrir has that skill.

"She's not special," Fenrir sneers, looking at me in disgust. "I can just use her body to get through the portal. I will become a god again to the foolish mortals, and they will worship *me*."

"You're not getting through the portal," Loki says, his voice eerily calm. "You are not worthy."

"If *she* can go through, all I need is her blood," Fenrir says. "I will bathe in it, and the portal will open before me."

Wind whips Loki's cloak out, and he unfastens it, letting the cloth drop dramatically away. Blades bloom in his hands.

"The fuck you will," he snarls.

CHAPTER 16
LOKI

know I have been a fool, but I have never felt it more strongly than I do right now, the weight of my failure crushing down on me as Fenrir sneers over the bodies of my council. My most trusted advisors.

My friends.

I will myself not to look at Sigyn especially — he had been with me from the beginning, from the opening of the portal and before, and now his glassy eyes stare unseeing into the clouded sky.

My grip tightens on my knives, shoulders tensing, breath coming in fogged huffs.

"Fenrir," I growl. "Stand down."

One final chance.

Though he does not deserve it.

But his actions are not his alone — they are mine.

Because I did not take seriously his boredom, because I brushed it off as a twitch he would outgrow, because I did not see how manic he was becoming, a general without a war.

These bodies. This death.

It is on me.

Fenrir laughs. The sound is grating and vile, and when his eyes fix on Faith again, I am a beast.

The way he looks at her, I know he is reading into her mind. I know he is seeing her memories, our lovemaking, her time here, and more — he will use it all against her. He will use it against me.

He made her scream. He made her *break*.

"Ah." Fenrir arches an eyebrow at me. "How does your cock fit in that tiny hole of hers? Perhaps I'll find out before I kill you and her both."

I move.

Fenrir expects it. He pulls a mighty ax out of a snowbank, not an illusion this time, white flurrying around it in a burst, and as I propel over the space between us, he is swinging.

Faith cries out. I flinch at the sound, a breath of a pause, but it is enough; Fenrir's swing grazes my midsection as my knives come down, one of my blades sinking into his shoulder, the other scraping off his armor.

I heave backwards, crimson blood spewing across the snow. Mine and Fenrir's both.

"Loki!" Snow crunches as Faith moves behind me. "*Loki* — "

"*Stay back*!" I bellow.

If she is injured.

If Fenrir hurts her in any way.

I do not know what kind of being I will become.

Fenrir cannot breach my mind with his feeble powers, but he must see the intent on my face. He lunges around me, ramming his shoulder into the newly opened wound across my chest. The sting of pain funnels into the knot of rage in my gut, and I lean into it, heaving my weight into Fenrir to stay him in place.

"You will not *touch her*," I snarl at him.

Fenrir laughs. But his ax is useless up close.

My knives, though?

My magic?

I flare one hand out wide. Fenrir and I are surrounded by a ring of Loki's, all armed, all feral.

I am king of the frost giants for a reason; I alone can make my illusions real.

I do not hesitate.

My illusions all dive at Fenrir, knives whirling.

Blood sprays. Fenrir grunts and stumbles back, disorientation heaving him left, right. His eyes flash to the Loki's, and I know he has lost sight of the real me. I feel a beat of relief — I have gotten the upper hand — before Fenrir's face goes utterly livid.

He knocks two Loki's aside, raises his ax, and throws it.

I follow the arc, breathless, and without thought, driven by the basest pulses of my instinct, I send another illusion out, creating a jutting bank of snow beneath Faith's feet. It hurls her bodily through the air.

Fenrir's ax had been aimed perfectly. It would have sliced her in two.

But I did not react quickly enough, and the spinning blade still manages to slice across her arm as she flies away.

Her blood flashes across the already blood-soaked snow. Her cry of pain rings in my ears, and all the sight around me goes red with fury.

Fenrir takes a step towards his ax, a grin on his face. He thinks he has won — he has her blood.

This will be the last thought he ever has.

I yank all of my illusions onto him. He expects mercy, as I have shown in the past. He expects me to be weak.

A dozen blades stab into his body simultaneously.

He does not even moan.

He yanks in a rattling breath, head dipping back, body seizing in an onslaught of pain.

I release the illusions, and as they vanish, Fenrir drops to his knees. His wide eyes lock on me, the real me, and there is his rage again, visceral and scalding.

"You won't . . . keep it . . . shut," he manages, blood dribbling down his chin. "If not me . . . then another . . . will open . . . we are gods, Loki. We are *gods*."

"No." I put one of my knives against Fenrir's bobbing throat. "On Earth, maybe. But we are home now."

Fenrir chuckles. It breaks off as I pierce his neck with my blade, and his body drops heavily to the side, snow encasing him.

I sheath my blades and bound across the snow to where Faith sits in a bank, cradling her arm.

Behind her, the portal flickers and heaves, brighter than I have seen it, as though it senses she is near.

I glare at it. *Not yet. You will not take her yet.*

"My Faith." I drop to my knees before her and gingerly take her arm in my hands. The cut is deep, and I grab a small medical pouch from the supplies I tied to my belt before we left.

"You're hurt, too — "

"I'm fine." I am too desperate to feel the pain.

Faith's eyes bore into me as I work.

I cannot look at her.

But I am breaking inside. These bodies around me — how easily she could have joined them —

"I am so sorry, my Faith," I tell her, my voice wavering. "This is my doing."

"No, it isn't. It was Fenrir. You aren't at fault for this."

I grit my jaw as I tie off a bandage around her arm. It will stop the bleeding, but she will need stitches, things I cannot do out here.

Things she could easily get in her world.

"It *is* my fault," I counter, "because I knew Fenrir was tempted. And I did nothing. But he is right — he will not open the portal, but the temptation remains for others. And as long as it remains . . ."

I cannot speak it.

"Your people aren't safe," Faith finishes. "If anyone from my world finds out you're here, you'll never know peace again."

That we could travel to each other's homes was a dream, I know.

I take her hands in mine. They are so small. Delicate and strong and I pull them to my mouth, press my lips into her palm.

"I can close it," I whisper into her skin, the secret hers alone. "I left it in its weakened state for the same greed that drove Fenrir — a chance of *maybe one day.* But I — "

"You have to close it. Fully." I cannot read any emotion in Faith's voice.

Finally, I look at her.

Her eyes are bloodshot, teary, and the sheer sadness on her face will be my doom. It is a sadness of resignation.

She has made her decision.

And I am torn asunder.

"I will close the portal behind you," I tell her.

I have to keep my people safe.

Even if it means breaking my own heart.

CHAPTER 17
FAITH

When I first woke up in Jotunheim, I thought I was dead. And then Loki became my heaven.

After, I thought it was a dream. A beautiful dream that I didn't want to wake from.

But now, Loki is before me, grief in his eyes, telling me it's time for me to wake up. To resurrect. To go back home.

Where my old life awaits me.

I search his eyes, looking for the answer to the question of me inside them.

But that answer has always been mine to choose.

My old life: studying archaeology I know now is alive and well and not ancient. How can I resign myself to finding long-buried mead halls and remnants of stone carved into a face that I kissed?

How can I look for altars to a god who knelt before me and worshipped my body as no man ever has before? How can I examine the old songs of deity praise for clues when he made me scream his praise in ecstasy?

My old life: an unsatisfying lover in every way, a man weaker than me in mind, weaker in bed than Loki. A mother who is dead, a father who has moved on from his old life, his old daughter, and created a family for himself that excludes me.

But also . . .

My friends, who became my family.

When Loki saw the dead body of his friend, Sigyn, he said his name as if it were a prayer. I say the names of my friends now. Dr. Phillips. Maya. Ursula. Cate. Marie. I say their names slowly, my voice a whisper that Loki cannot hear as I step away, closer to the portal. They are each a reason for me to go back to my world, my time, my reality.

But when I say their names, I say them as a farewell.

I don't touch the portal, even though it is just in front of me. I try to look through the swirling colors, to see into the world I once believed was my only possibility.

I turn to Loki instead, and see a different possibility.

"I don't want to go," I say simply, the truth ringing with the clarity of a struck bell.

Loki's face shifts from sorrowful to carefully masked. "You don't?" he asks in an even monotone.

I shake my head. "I agree with you — you have to break the portal. If I fell through, others may come looking for me. They may come through. And Jotunheim must be protected. *You* must be protected."

Loki's eyes are flat; he is being so careful to show no emotion. But I have come to know him well.

"If it is best for your people or . . . or for you, I will go," I continue. "And you can break the portal after me. But if you'll have me, I will stay. And you can break the portal now."

"You would stay here forever?" Loki asks in careful measures.

"I would stay here with you," I say.

Loki's mask starts to fall away, and I see for the first time the emotion he had been trying to hide: hope. He hoped that I would stay, but he did not dare ask the sacrifice of me. I think before this moment, I would have said he was being silly; it is not a sacrifice to have one's dreams fulfilled. But there is a pang in my chest as the weight of what I'm choosing settles on my shoulders. There *is* sacrifice here. I can give up some things of my past life easily enough, but the love I have for my sisters in education is real, and their loss is bittersweet.

But I know that the love I share with my friends is real, because I know that they would encourage me to do this thing, to follow my heart into a fate beyond my wildest imaginations, to fulfill the needs of my mind, body, and soul here in Jotunheim. To not hold myself back for them.

"Only . . ." I say. Loki's brows twist in concentration, and I feel certain he would do anything I ask of him in this moment. "Would it be possible for me to get a message to my sisters?"

I tap the pockets of my jacket, pulling out the pencil and waterproof paper that I carried for field research. I feel another pang in my chest — this coat and the little pad of paper were gifts from Dr. Phillips. And I'm going to use them to tell her goodbye forever.

The people who walked the Earth when Loki and the gods of Asgard ruled knew runes, but Loki watches curiously as I scrawl out a note in English to my loved ones.

Everyone — I am fine. Better than fine.
I know this will be hard to believe, but I have found
everything — EVERYTHING — I was looking for. But I
am also not going to be able to come back to you.

Please know that I love you all, and that I am well and unbelievably happy. My only sadness is the knowledge that I will not be able to say farewell in person.

I pause, reading over my words. I know that this is not enough. If Elanor or Josie left behind a similar message, I would worry that they had been kidnapped or fell into a cult or something. But I struggle to find the balance between the words I need to say and what I must keep hidden. I can't tell them about Jotunheim or Loki.

Instead, I write in Old Norse across the bottom a quick note for Dr. Phillips, hoping it is enough to convince her.

It is all real. Loki is real.
And I am choosing a life with him that is not nothing.

It will have to be enough. But I feel certain Dr. Phillips will remember the way I called my old boyfriend nothing, how my life had felt like nothing before I left. It's not much of a coded message, but I hope it's enough to convince her that all is well.

I fold the message up tightly, forming an envelope and write on the front:

If this message is found,

please ensure it gets to Dr. Amie Phillips.

I add in the address of the university.

I'm not sure of my chances of this note being found. I fell through the lake on the island and woke up here; my paper is waterproof, but not forever. And how can I hope for one piece of paper to make it through?

The wind blows, bitterly cold. "Loki," I say, an idea occurring to me, "I can put my message to my friends inside my coat. I think they will find it."

I slip the paper into the waterproof pocket inside the coat, then take it off, zipping it up and folding it tightly. The neon orange puffy material is my best bet at the message being found.

I hold it up to him, and he nods. "This will be found," he says, rubbing one of his blue fingers over the bright cloth. I'm not sure if he means the vivid color will stand out, or if he intends to add some of his magic to ensure it's discovered. "May I?"

I pass the bundled coat to him, and he hurtles it through the portal. It blends in the swirling light and then disappears.

"Are you ready?" Loki asks. "Are you sure?"

I nod. I have never been more certain.

Loki picks up his woolen cloak and drapes it around my shivering shoulders. I relish in the heat it carries from his skin, the smell that clings to the cloth. I'm not sure what will destroy the portal — I expect some sort of magic, truth be told, but instead, Loki picks up a boulder and smashes it into the portal rift. The rocks crumble and the portal drifts into nothingness.

It's done.

Loki turns, not even a sheen of sweat at the way he picked up a boulder. "My Faith," he says gently, crossing to me.

Despite his cloak, I'm still cold. Loki picks me up, wrapping his strong arms around me. I suppose I should be nervous about this choice. I will never again go back to the world I was born into.

But this is the world I always wanted.

I cling to Loki. This is the man I always wanted.

"My queen," he whispers against my neck, sending a wave of heat over my body.

This is the love I always wanted.

CHAPTER 18
LOKI

Everything will be perfect. Because of Faith.

I watch her from the rear of the feast hall, a grin on my face. That grin has not waned since we returned to the palace days ago, and I have been enraptured utterly in watching Faith commit to her life here.

To our life here.

She instructs a group of workers where to place baskets of greenery. Decorations aplenty fill this hall already, but not yet enough; Faith is pulled away by another arrival of still more, but dried flower petals now, fragrant things she instructs to be sprinkled on tables. Another servant arrives and touches her elbow — Tove.

I push up from the wall, neck craning for the package in Tove's arms.

Faith bends over it, her face softening, and I can feel the awe in her sigh even across the room. It is the gown Faith will wear tonight, one I have not been allowed to see, and as she and Tove exclaim over it, I find my curiosity roiling.

But the moment I take a step forward, deeper into the room, Faith's head swivels and her eyes pin on me.

She tips her head, eyebrow lifting, and I freeze, hands out, caught.

She points behind me with a haughtiness that hardens my cock. *"Go,"* she mouths.

One of her many insistences — we adhere to every tradition, including the rituals of maidenhood for her and a sword ceremony for me, things meant to separate us.

She has been committed to keeping us apart until tonight.

I glower at her now.

Faith's lower lip catches between her teeth, and it is a great show of restraint on my part that I do not dive across the room and pin her to a table.

She whispers something to Tove, who eyes me and shakes her head. Faith goes back to her preparations as Tove crosses the room to me.

"Begone with you!" the weaver swats my arm.

"The men are gathered and waiting, did you know? They are on the steps already!"

I reach for the bundled fabric in her arms, a rich hunter green with gold embroidery. "Only a moment longer; let me see the — "

Tove swats me again.

I pull back in mock offense. "I am king here and will not be dismissed so carelessly."

"*Begone* or Faith has informed me that she will extend this separation beyond tonight." Tove points a harsh finger at me. "A bride in no way guarantees wedding night favors to the groom."

A beat.

"Is that so?" My eyes flash back to Faith, who is smiling to herself, deliberately not looking at me.

I twitch my fingers. Unseen to all around, I create an illusion just beneath her skirts. It is a mimic of my fingers as I stroke up, and I see Faith's body jerk like a lightning strike as my illusion slips into her folds.

She is wet. Wet and warm, and my hard cock throbs.

Faith swings towards me again. *"Loki!"* she mouths, then throws her hands up and rushes away, but her parting exasperated smile will hold me over for hours yet.

She is close to breaking, I know; not nearly as close as I am, but still.

"Fine." I sigh mightily at Tove. "I am banished. Do look after my betrothed while I am gone. I hear you are to lead her maidenhood ritual?"

"Indeed, my king. She will be most cared for." There is true affection in Tove's voice, enough that I leave the hall with no hesitation, no worry for my Faith in the least.

I was not the only one overjoyed at Faith's decision to stay.

As I leave, I see smiles on my people of light and joy. Our days had been joyous before, but now they are *new,* new not only because of my impending marriage to Faith, but because of the rituals and customs she has rebirthed. She has breathed new life into our every day, and I feel all sense of stagnation and boredom slipping away.

When I push out onto the top steps of the palace, there indeed is gathered a group of frost giant men, all outfitted in war paint and impressive leather armor and strapping swords. They joke and laugh in the crisp cold air, and I pause for a moment, watching their camaraderie.

My heart breaks that Sigyn is not among them. That I could not create this sort of energy before greed such as Fenrir's took lives.

But I did not create this sort of energy — it was all Faith. Long had we forgotten a groom's ritual of the sword ceremony, where I must pursue a hidden sword across the tundra with my men in tow, and the very idea of such a thing has the men buzzing with eagerness.

Faith gave us this. The same as she gives us the preparations in the hall, and her maidenhood ritual, and all the other plans for Jotunheim's growth she has told me of these past days. Her presence here is a breath of fresh air, a pierce of gilded light in the dark; she is not merely my love, but Jotunheim's salvation.

I breathe deeply of the cool air and jog to meet up with the men.

———

I am not used to my bedchamber being empty.

Faith dresses with her women elsewhere, and though I know I have but moments until I am reunited with her again — and it has only been twelve short hours of separation, truly; I am insatiable — being alone in my room, tying a belt around my waist in silence, has me feeling too much like the old days.

So when the door opens, I am at once relieved.

"Is it time?" I turn, expecting my councilors —

But it is Faith who slips into the room.

I do not even question why she is here, nor point out that she is breaking her own inflicted rules.

In an instant, I am across the room, my hands seizing her waist, lifting her, pinning her to the door. My mouth is on hers ravenously, tongue stroking the inside of her mouth as though she is frosty water, and I am dying of thirst.

"Loki!" she gasps, dissolving in a giggle when I nuzzle her neck and nip the skin there. "*Loki* — oh, *stop*! It hasn't been that long."

"Long enough," I moan into her skin. "Every moment is too long, my Faith."

I press my knee between her legs, holding her there, freeing my hands to roam.

I pull back, startled. She is dressed already, and I take in her gown, the tight pull of the laces that enhance her breasts and hips, the delicate embroidery of mistletoe and horns and repeating patterns along the hems. Her hair is an array of braids and curls all pinned back, her face softened by blush and a gloss on her lips I taste now, berries of some sort.

"Faith," I growl, and then my face is back against her neck. "You are divinity incarnate. I will take you first in this gown, pressed against the door of the feast hall, where you will have to stifle your screams lest all our people know precisely how you sound in ecstasy."

"Oh my *god*, Loki — " Faith melts a little, her body going lax to my ministrations, and I snake a hand up her smooth thigh, lifting the dress higher, higher —

She mewls, head lolling back, and grabs my hand. "This isn't — " a gasp, a fight for breath. "This isn't why I came."

"No?" I suck her earlobe into my mouth.

"N-no — *fuck*, Loki, I swear — "

"Hmm. You are wet, my Faith — I think you are lying. Why did you come? You knew I would not be able to resist you."

My thumb is knuckle-deep in her cunt, and I feel it contract around me, enough that I stumble, dizzying, my cock aching to be lodged inside her.

Faith's chest and cheeks are stained red. She rolls her head up to look at me, her eyes gone dark and heady.

"Maybe it is why I came," she whispers. "But not like *this*."

She pushes her small hand in the center of my chest, and I feel our size differences fully then. Her, so small; me, towering over her, encompassing all light and space.

But she knows I am hers entirely.

I back up, lowering her to the ground, and when she pushes harder, I sink to my knees.

It is a natural stance with her, prostrate, beseeching, worshipping.

Faith reaches into a pocket on her gown. "One tradition I am most looking forward to," she starts, her hand fisted around something. "Is the hand-fasting."

She lets her hand open and a ribbon of deepest red dangles from her fingers.

This is a tradition my people still employed. Two people allow their hands to be knotted together in symbol of their union. It is how Faith and I will be married in only moments now.

My eyes go to the ribbon. Then back to Faith, where she watches me with deep intent.

I tip my head. "Oh?"

Faith stretches the ribbon between her hands. "Tove presented this to me, and my first thought was: is it strong enough?" She tugs on it. "How awful that would be. If, during the ceremony, the whole ribbon just . . . *snapped.*"

"Awful, truly." My eyes are fixed on Faith. On her pink cheeks. The slit of cleavage peeking through her dress.

"Your duty as groom," she tells me, "is to test the ribbon's resilience."

My eyebrow lifts along with a slow smile. "I will

help in any way you ask. This ceremony will be the product of your dreams."

I lift my wrists, presenting them to her, fighting a feral smile as she slowly loops the ribbon around and around.

When I am bound, Faith leans close, her lips ghosting over mine.

"Now," she says, and I can taste her words, a honeyed sweetness on her breath, "stay still. You only get to watch."

She backs up, lifting her dress to slip her hand beneath, and I know she is touching herself by the way her eyelids flutter.

I strain against the ribbon. It is soft and delicate; I could snap it easily.

"Faith," I say her name, a low growl. "You play a dangerous game. I am a man starving, and you come here, presenting a feast, saying I cannot take a single bite?"

She grins at me. It is all temptation.

"Yes, Loki," she says. She lifts her skirt so I can see her fingers plunge deeply into her cunt. They come out, slick with her moisture, and when she traces a circle around her clit, I hear myself growl. "That is exactly what I am saying. What are you going to do about it, god of mischief, king of the frost giants?"

Now my smile is feral. My very being, untamed.

A myriad of images flashes through my mind. Taking her against the door as I promised; hauling her bodily from the feast room the moment we are wed; throwing her down on a table and fucking her senseless while wine is poured and songs play.

Or insisting she retie me, as she has now, and letting my illusions use her body until she is sated and limp with pleasure. How long can she last with them? We have made it just over an hour so far before she moaned with sensitivity and exhaustion.

Perhaps, tonight, it will be two hours. Three.

Perhaps, tonight, her punishment will be four illusions of me. Five.

"Bring yourself to climax, my queen," I tell her, "and tonight, after we are wed, you will find out precisely what sort of god you have unleashed."

EPILOGUE

The package on Dr. Phillips's desk looks like it's been to hell and back. The box has no sharp corners, each one dented and crushed. The packaging tape that surrounds the box is thicker than the actual cardboard, and Dr. Phillips is careful with her knife as she cuts open the layers.

The note at the top is written in blocky English on a weather-worn index card. It's succinct and to the point:

This jacket was found with your information attached.
It was <u>under</u> the lake's ice.

"Under the ice," Dr. Phillips says to the empty, dim room. If it disturbed her to know that her student's protective gear had been found under a thick layer of ice, she did not show it in her careful, measured movements and schooled face.

Putting the note to the side, Dr. Phillips withdrew a bright orange arctic-grade coat. The same one she'd gifted to her student, Faith Beck, before she left on her expedition after graduation. Dr. Phillips's hand goes instinctively to the weatherproof pocket on the inside lining.

As she suspected, there is another note inside, this one written in Faith's hurried scrawl.

Dr. Phillips reads it through once, twice, a third time.

A slow smile spreads across her face.

Dr. Phillips jumps at the sharp knock on her door. A quick glance at her clock confirms that her next thesis mentee — Josie Granat — has arrived for her appointment. Dr. Phillips stuffs the coat back into the box and kicks the bedraggled tape-covered cardboard under her desk. She takes both notes — the one on the index card and the one Faith had written — and puts them in her desk drawer, to be filed later.

Through the frosted glass window in her door, Dr. Phillips can see the outline of her student, waiting.

Dr. Phillips pulls down a series of Ancient Greek

mythologies from her bookshelf, lining them along the edge of her desk. Josie, she knows, has already read all the texts, most of them in the original Greek. There is little left to teach her.

Or, at least, little left that Dr. Phillips can teach her.

It is time for Josie to get some hands-on research, and Dr. Phillips can only hope that her pitch to go to the Mediterranean will be met with enthusiasm from her bookish and travel leery student.

It was easy enough to leave the trail for Faith to follow, although, of course, she had to be the one to take the plunge. Literally.

Fate will guide this student's journey, too.

She turns to face the door. "Come in!" she calls, and the door opens.

This is not the end of the Gods & Monsters series.
Join us for the next sexy adventure:
DEMON PRINCE HADES

BONUS MATERIAL

We want to thank you so much for sharing in this adventure with us! This book has been a labor of love, and it's made better by sharing with readers like you. Our newsletter will always keep you up-to-date with the latest sexy releases, and signing up will get you a free short story! You can subscribe at https://rarebooks. substack.com

Please consider leaving a review—they help new writers more than almost anything else, and ensure that we can keep writing this series.

What's next in Gods & Monsters? Each story in the series will follow a different member of the Study Group as they discover how the gods, monsters, myths, and legends they read about in books are in reality. Every novel in this shared-world series is a sexy adventure you won't want to miss!

Our next story will feature a new heroine and a new god . . . one who certainly is more monstrous than worshipful . . .

Never miss a thing at https://rarebooks. substack.com

READ A SAMPLE OF THE MAGICIAN

n addition to the Gods & Monsters Series, Liza and Natasha co-wrote the Heroes & Villains Series. While Gods & Monsters takes your favorite myths and legends and adds a sexy, fun twist, the Heroes & Villains series did the same thing with classic superhero stories.

Sign up for our newsletter and get a free novella featuring a very sexy encounter plus access to loads more free stories and bonuses.

The Heroes & Villains series is entirely complete, and available individually or in bound collections. Liza and Natasha were inspired to write the Gods & Monsters series in part because fans loved the iteration of Loki they portrayed in *Magician*. Each story in the series can be read out of order, so please enjoy a peek at our first Loki now!

Magic bursts from his palms. The flowers in the penthouse shift, the petals growing larger, more pointed. Like Asgardian blooms. The floor shifts from wood paneling to gray stone, the same floor as the balcony outside of Loki's room in the Asgardian palace.

My gaze flicks to Loki's. I realize that he lost control—his magic gave him what he wanted, without him directing it.

He wants that night back.

The night, before, when we had nothing but love between us.

No—that's not right. There were secrets between us then. My secrets. The plans of my father.

But…there are no secrets now. There's just us.

I am exposed. Not just my body, but my past.

And he still wants me.

And I want him to have me.

"Rora," he breathes, that tell-tale smirk of his that shows me how tempted he is.

"I don't deserve you. This." I look around. "I don't deserve flowers."

A frown mars his gorgeous face. "You deserve more than I can ever give you." He reaches for my hand, feeling the heavy ring on my finger, the only thing I still wear. The emerald is breathtaking, like the deepest flecks of green in his eyes.

His hand slides down my finger, around my wrist. He encircles my wrist like a manacle. My pulse quickens.

"Tell me a word," he says. "A safe word. You speak that word, and everything will stop. It will be our word alone, and when we use that word, we know the other is being true. Always." His voice is so earnest, so sincere.

I lick my lips, thinking. His eyes watch my lips hungrily.

"Guardian," I say finally. It is what he is to me.

"Guardian." And then he grabs my wrist, yanking me around, spinning me so quickly off my feet that I nearly fall. He catches me, though—without releasing my hand. Pain shoots up my arm—not much, but it's not a comfortable position.

"Say it," he demands.

"Guardian."

He releases me. I stagger from the loss of his touch.

"That's our word now," he says. A promise. "Would you like me to go? Or would you like company tonight?"

I would like company, always, if that company is you.

"Stay," I whisper. "It is, after all, our wedding night."

His grin is absolutely feral. "On your knees, Rora," he says imperiously.

———

The Heroes & Villains series is fully available right now! All your favorite superheroes, recast in the naughtiest ways…

ALSO BY LIZA PENN & NATASHA LUXE

The Heroes and Villains Series:

All books also available in paperback

Prequel Novella: Origin (*free for subscribers*)

Book 1: Nemesis

Newsletter short story "Fly With Us"

Book 2: Alter Ego

Book 3: Secret Sanctum

Book 4: Magician

Book 5: Thunder

Book 6: Goddess

Phase 1: Books 1-3 + Bonus Content

Phase 2: Books 4-6 + Bonus Content

Also by Natasha Luxe

Celebrity Crush Series

Club Reverie Series

Also by Liza Penn:

As Above Romance Fantasy Serial

Hotel Ever After Series

ABOUT THE AUTHORS

Liza Penn and Natasha Luxe are a pair of author friends with bestselling books under different names. They joined forces—like all the best superheroes do—for the greater good.

You can keep up with them at their newsletter. Located at rarebooks.substack.com, they often feature links to freebies and bonus material.

For more information about all their books and extra goodies for readers, check out their website at thepennandluxe.com.